# Listen

# Listen

Francesca G. Varela

FIRST EDITION TRADE PAPERBACK
ISBN: 978-1-938846-52-6 (PBK)

www.owlhousebooks.com
www.homeboundpublications.com
or visit the author at www.francescavarela.com

Interior and Cover Designed by Leslie M. Browning
Cover Images by: © Watercolor Bird by Radiocat © Feathers by Inna Ogando
© Blue Watercolor background by Hofhauser © Green Fern by Juicy Bloom

10 9 8 7 6 5 4 3 2 1

Homebound Publications is committed to ecological stewardship. We greatly value the natural environment and invests in environmental conservation. Our books are printed on paper with chain of custody certification from the Forest Stewardship Council, Sustainable Forestry Initiative, and the Program for the Endorsement of Forest Certification.

# Chapter One

"Haven't you had enough of this yet?"

"Had enough of what? Of my life? This is my life now, Hallie."

"I know. That's what I mean."

We waited for the silence to break. Sometimes, without us trying, music would work its way in; it was a string between us, always tied.

"How the hell did you get a piano up here?" My sister glared at the corner. "You don't even have a phone, but you have a Steinway?"

"It came with the house." I wiped a drop of spit from my lip.

I jumped over the creaking wood floor to the black bench. With forced lightness I began a Mozart sonata. C major. What I really needed was Chopin, but Hallie hated Chopin. She didn't get him; couldn't find the melody.

My fingers pecked the keys. It was staccato, charming, just right for the classical era. This one was memorized, so I looked at the window and the rain. My hands knew what to do.

The first movement was only halfway through, and she knew it, but Hallie stood up. I finished the measure. Silently, I turned the cover down over the shining white keys.

She watched the floor. Her breathing was so loud I could see it.

"Sounds good, right? The tone? Too bad you don't have your violin." I frowned, fingers folded in my lap. "We could've done a duet like we used to."

"I haven't played the violin in years, May. I wasn't good enough for an orchestra or anything. I told you about the auditions. It was going nowhere." She leaned against the bookcase. "And I'm not a composer like you. Never have been."

"But, Hallie, you're so good at it. You play with so much emotion, everyone always said so . . ." The tea water whistled. I moved toward the kitchen. "You haven't really given up, have you?"

The kitchen always seemed warmer than the other three rooms, all of which were wrapped in rich wood. We sat at the table with our dark blue mugs. Steam poured from the metal pot, and I inhaled the cinnamon smells that came with it.

"You really think you're gonna make any money off of this?" Hallie sighed.

"Of course not. But I got this place for free, you know." I blew into my cup and stole its warmth for my hands. It sustained me, in that moment. "What've I got to lose?"

"Who was it, again? Who owned it?"

"Some friend of Grandma's. It was his vacation home. I don't even remember meeting him. Apparently he heard me play before he died, and left the cabin to me in his will. As a place to compose. It's perfect —"

"Being isolated up here is perfect?" she interrupted.

"Yes. And the forest. And the piano. All of it."

Hesitantly, I touched my lips to the rim of the mug. Hallie did the same. She tilted her head back and took an impatient sip. Her mouth curled up as she swallowed the heat. We leaned back in our chairs, crossing our legs. I finally let the tea roll over my tongue.

"None of us like you being here. Mom and Dad are convinced you're going to be killed by a murderer or something and none of us will even know. That kind of thing happens ... anything could happen to you, and there would be no one to help. We can't even call to check on you. We have to drive two hours straight on winding back roads—"

"You don't have to."

"Oh my god, May, yes we do. We would all go crazy if we didn't know what was happening up here. And what are you even gonna get out of all this? You know? Look, why don't you just come home, down to civilization. Get a job as a teacher or something. There's a big demand for music teachers. You can even compose at home until you save up."

I rested my cup on the table with a steady fist. I studied her face. Wide cheekbones and a strong chin. Her brown eyes were just like mine, only hers were never free from sparkling eye shadow. She was so much prettier than me.

"Just listen to this, listen to what I've been coming up with."

I rushed to the piano. Out it came, all the sorrows I had ever felt.

"May."

It was red and it was restless. Heavy and swirling and crushing everything around it.

"May."

The world disappeared. A new one opened.

"May! Fine! Fine, I'll leave, if you're just going to ignore me."

I stepped into it. I was swaying, floating. I was movement.

"Who's even going to hear you play?"

Hallie slammed the door, and a minute later her car roared. My song came to its sad, long end.

Then I started in on Chopin.

# Chapter Two

I was twenty-four when I moved into the cabin. There were solar-panels on the roof and a full set of furniture. After adding a nice quilt to the bed, my clothes to the armoire, toiletries to the cabinet, and my music books to the shelf, it felt wholly my own.

My days were carefree. It was just music; music and nature. I had no errands, no bills. All I really had to pay for was food. In the summer I got along well enough on wild berries. They grew everywhere, especially along the stream.

One day I followed that stream, and I traced its journey back to a clear pond. I laid next to it as the sun made its journey. Ferns brushed against my hair, moss against my elbows. On my knees, I stared into the pool. My own eyes looked back. Not only that, they looked down and into the Earth's mouth.

Reliance on the forest allowed me to know it. When the forest breathed, so did I. Each day I walked a fresh path among the Douglas firs. I looked for new things, for yew trees, for huckleberries; for potato bugs and deer tracks.

My favorite thing was to watch the wind comb through the trees. Sometimes I stretched my arms up as it swept by. I was never quite tall enough to touch the same air as the treetops.

The birds were; their flight made them as tall as the sky. Chickadees came in little, hopping, groups, climbing ever higher. I loved their frantic songs, and I tried to mimic them. A musician has no better inspiration than birdsongs.

I've been a musician for as long as I can remember. There's always been music in my head.

We had an old piano in our living room, a beige upright. It was my grandmother's, then my mom's, and when my fingers were on it, it was mine.

Its voice was tinny. The lowest keys stuck, and the highest were always out of tune. Mom didn't play. She just liked how it looked, sitting there next to the armchair.

Rain was best for playing, especially when a little sunlight fought its way through. The hollow sound of the piano broke through the window and encircled the sky. Clouds were struck by the light, eagerly painted deep and dark.

Each piece of music was my imaginary world. At five

years old I taught myself to read sheet music, at least the basics of it. Then I began to create. It was effortless; the notes cycled through me from the air. It took awhile for my parents to realize it.

My young improvisations were mistaken for the work of Bach, or even Haydn, by my unmusical parents.

Once my parents recognized my talent, they signed me up for lessons at the neighborhood studio. My sister is three years older, but I was the first one to learn. Her interest didn't come until that Christmas, when I had already been taking lessons for four months.

I flew downstairs that morning, early enough that there was still more shadow than light. I was shivering without my robe or slippers. A curved outline against the window's glow held a fat, red ribbon. Blindly, I ran my hand against the side.

Even though my parents and Hallie were still asleep, I sat down. I unveiled the keys, and, still sightless, I began.

One by one they stumbled downstairs. Mom's blond hair was in a smooth braid, Hallie's in a frizzed puff. Dad's narrow eyes were barely open. Unable even to fake grumpiness on such an occasion, they plugged in the tree's lights and listened to me play.

Although it was old, the keys had held up well and the pedals didn't squeak. And the way it hummed . . .

magnificent. Everyone knows that older pianos have a better sound. Newer ones must be broken in.

Later, when I propped up the top, Hallie sat mesmerized, watching the hammers hit the strings. It didn't matter whether it was my piano or hers. There it was, in our house, and we could both play it.

"I want to learn," she told our parents.

So she joined me at the music studio for group lessons. Every Tuesday from five to six. I was one of the youngest, and certainly the best. Hallie had trouble reading the bass clef and counting out time. I moved on to private lessons. She was held back a level. Within two years Hallie had given up piano in favor of a new instrument.

"Violin is way harder than piano," she declared from the velvet armchair, slicing through my practicing with the shrieks of her rented violin." Anyone can learn to play the piano."

It was painful at first to hear her work out the scratchy pitches. Eventually, though, her melodies grew sweet. We ceased to compete. Instead, we complemented each other.

"Let's hear a duet, girls." My father handed us one of Beethoven's sonatas for piano and violin. He smiled at us, his delicate mouth reminiscent of my own.

Within a few hours I was proficient. My sight-reading was already fluent. Hallie took a few days, but finally we came together.

Our parents sat on the couch as we performed. Leaning eagerly forward, they stared at us as though they couldn't look away. Both of us messed up. We stumbled, our timing diverged. Hallie ignored all dynamics in favor of *fortissimo,* the loudest. But my mom's hazel eyes were almost wet.

"Where did this talent come from, Ned?" she asked my dad, her voice falling low.

He bared his teeth and shook his head jokingly. "They most certainly didn't get it from us."

To me, my future was obvious. Concert pianist and composer. Maybe a piano teacher in my old age. That was just about the only steady job music could offer. The idea of having something consistent to fall back on soothed my parents, so they supported me.

In the meantime, I was a child. My freest and happiest moments were at the piano or outside. Our house was old, and on enough land to be called a farm.

When it wasn't raining I would pick wildflowers in the meadow behind the woods. White and yellow and purple; every color too beautiful to be named a weed. With their hairy stems tucked in my hair, I would spin in circles. Next to the little pond I danced my own ballet, music forever turning within me.

There was a particular cluster of trees that I called my nest. It was a blanket of moss and horsetails bordered by cedar limbs. Crouching among the folded maple leaves, I wondered about the universe. What it was inside of. I dreamt up stories with their own soundtracks, or crushed centipedes with twigs, just to see what was within.

Some days I would climb trees in the old orchard, especially when there were apples or plums waiting at the top. It always smelled like the ripest fruit, their scents gathering upon the moist earth. In summer those treats would leave sugar upon my lips. I had to jump down before ants crawled up the trunk and onto my hands.

My friends at school were few but strong. They lived farther in town, so I was usually alone. Hallie played games with me at first. She grew out of them quickly and early, turning away from me to paint her fingernails.

Then I was alone with my imaginary worlds, spending entire summers beneath the sky. My mom would call me to the back door at lunch, and hand me a peanut-butter and honey sandwich. I always ate it sprawled upon the wild grass, watching whatever clouds swam by.

After the pink sunset I played piano until dinner, and again afterwards. I played for as long as I could before everyone else went to sleep. I wrote music inspired by the pond, by the fenced-in horse at the end of our dirt road, by every season that brought its own green beauty.

While my fingers leapt I let my mind wander. I relived the joys of the day; like ripping up ivy-root and tying it on to a stick to make a fishing pole, or leaping through the meadow, pretending to fly.

Occasionally I wrote down my compositions on lined paper, but that took too long. Usually I just kept it all in my head.

In high school I began to realize my mediocrity in all things but music. I wasn't popular, I wasn't antisocial. I was just forgotten. Normal, I guess. I had only a handful of close friends; Jessie, Ashley, and Sarah.

They weren't into classical music, so I rarely mentioned the piano. According to them, all Beethoven did was wave a stick around.

Instead we went to movies on the weekends, had sleepovers, listened to mindless popular music. We went to homecoming and prom as a group, making dates of scrawny boys who we rarely talked to in class. As long as we went, our social standing was maintained.

Half my classmates were partiers who stole beer and smoked pot. My innocence was preserved far longer than most of theirs. Even *I* could recognize that.

I never had a real boyfriend in high school. It was obvious that I was neither beautiful nor hideous, because either way people would've commented on it. I would've known. Boys didn't come after me; I had to work to gain their attention. Silence and indifference meant I was average.

That was alright, because I knew my talent. I knew the course I wanted to take through life.

In eighth grade I had my first kiss. It was the last class of the day, on the last day of school. The teacher left the room for a minute. Then I heard the nasally voice of the boy behind me.

"I dare you to kiss someone."

Half a moment passed, then there were numb lips on mine. It passed in an instant, dry and timid.

"Why'd you pick *her?*"

"She was the closest!" The blond boy jumped behind me, wiping his mouth with his wrist.

The teacher came back in, painfully oblivious. No one else even seemed to notice, except those two boys. I couldn't say anything. If I made a big deal about it, they would know my first kiss had been stolen. And who hadn't been kissed by eighth grade?

So I sat there in the wooden desk. I dreamed a dripping, minor melody, and that night I let it go.

Piano was another world to school. I kept them separate. My grades were low B's, high C's. Maybe if I had studied more they would've been better. Any spare time I had was spent visiting the forest, or practicing Chopin's waltzes.

Hallie had perfect grades, and was lead violin in the school orchestra. There was no place for a pianist in the school's music program.

"Is Hallie the smart one?" I was often asked.

I never knew how to respond. Was she? My mind, I felt, was different. Open to another realm.

Despite my normalcy, or maybe because of it, I longed for greatness.

One day, around third grade, I was kneeling in my forested nest. It was fall, and the trees were dying again. Only the vine maples had begun to blush orange. The sun was a bundled knot behind thick clouds, barely lending warmth. I was in my heavy, blue coat.

It began to mist. I could see it beyond the forest. Not one drop of water fell on my hair. The wind sprayed the trees, but not me. Under the canopy, the ferns became waves around me; swaying, rushing. Under the canopy, I was safe.

In that moment, I stood. My feet sank into the eternally damp dirt. For some reason, a sadness had come over me. I would never be younger, I realized. I don't know why, but the darkness made that suddenly apparent. I knew I wasn't a little kid anymore. Each second I would grow older, until, one day, I would die. Really die. It wasn't something that happened only in movies, but to everyone. It would be darkness. Like the densest sleep we don´t remember upon waking.

Even as a child it bothered me to know I wasn´t immortal. No afterlife had been promised me by my religionless parents. The only way to cheat death was to be known; to be remembered.

So I sought immortality through composition. If my music was played beyond my death, I wouldn´t really be dead. My music was part of me. It was a piece of my inner life. In each note I would live again.

But . . . how?

My college prospects were limited to in-state, because of costs. So I chose one four hours from home, near the mountains. It was old and small, but had the best music program.

Hallie had gone to another university, in the city. She wanted to be a teacher. Violin came second to her, almost like an afterthought.

But I held passion in each breath. The world was powerful, sweeping music. She just couldn´t hear it. It was only there for me.

# Chapter Three

Three long, terrible days had passed without playing. I felt nearly dead, and my first lesson was in half an hour.

I was all settled in to my studio apartment, right next to the campus. It had a bed, bathroom, and the tiniest of kitchens. There were no dorms at the college, and who could possibly be my roommate? I knew no one.

The school's practice rooms were across campus. I tried to get an apartment closer to them, but they were too expensive. It was a small school. The walk wasn't bad.

We were on the other side of the mountains, the dry side. It was a flat, brown plain that stretched on forever. As we crossed over the pass, I had watched the trees change instantly from firs to pines, then to sparse grassland. My forests were gone, lurking in the snow-trimmed shadow behind me.

There was only sky. That was the beauty of the landscape; it contained nothing, setting the horizon free.

I hurried along the pathways in my sandals. The air stroked my throat, smoky from distant wildfires. Even from behind its thin veil, the sun threw down heat. How could this be September?

My breath was heavy from rushing. Finally I came to the square, bulky music building. From outside the black doors I could already hear a cello's yawn, a drum's hiss. Skipping every other step, I jogged toward the doorway they'd shown me at orientation. The only thing stopping me from bolting were the ever-present eyes.

There they were. Neat little rooms encased in soundproof glass. Willing my chest to calm itself, I peeked into each one. Violinist. Pianist. Singer. I tugged on my jean shorts and pulled up my orange tank top. Twenty minutes until my lesson. My new teacher's first impression needed to be me at my best.

The old lights twinkled slightly. Licking my lips, I knocked twice on the door nearest me. I could already see a brown-haired boy playing an upright piano inside. He paused, his fingers hovering. Shuffling my feet on the stained, dark carpet, I stuck my smiling head in.

"Sorry." I threw my thick hair over my shoulder. "Um, I was really hoping I could use this room, just for, like, fifteen minutes before my lesson. I'm a music major, and I haven't practiced in a few days, and all the practice rooms are full."

He stretched his upper body toward me from the bench. I felt bad for thinking it, but it was obvious that he wasn't handsome. At all. Around his dense blue eyes were purple sacks. His ears stuck out, his skin was uneven. Beneath the yellow lighting his brow appeared weighty atop his receding chin.

An ugly boy must be thrilled to earn attention from any girl. Of course he'd let me use the room. It was, sadly, perfect.

"I'm a music major too," he grunted. His voice was like gravel, like pebbles scraping through water.

He set down his long fingers and played one of Chopin's Nocturnes, of all things. An easy piece. But, then . . . it was like I had never heard it before. Something new, soaring.

I wanted to sink away from his turned head. Why did he have to show off? Couldn't he just give me the room?

But I couldn't leave. It was Chopin.

Not only that, it took hold of me. It was as though I was watching the night sky, all the stars in the universe. Like I was lying there below the milky way's jewels, my head resting against sleeping dandelions. Red glimpses of alien worlds. Then the clouds would come and rain, not down, but up . . .

"It's all yours," he said as he stood. I realized, waking from my trance, that he'd been playing from memory.

"Too late," I muttered, wrapping my fists around the handle of my tote. "Only five minutes until my lesson now."

For a moment he stared at me. Then his round cheeks tightened. He slammed back down onto the bench.

"Well, have a good lesson, then." He nodded, eyes to the floor. "I should've let you play."

"No, it's okay. That was really good." I had to say, because I meant it. Even though I wanted to be mad at him, I couldn't be. "I'm glad I got to hear it."

By the time I turned around, music was already seeping out from behind the glass door.

I jumped down the hallway, wringing my stiff fingers. Not only was I going to be out of practice, I was going to be late if I couldn't find the right room. My shoulder ached from my bag, heavy with sheet music.

Sighing, I followed the room numbers. III . . . 112, there. I knocked softly on the closed door. Instantly, it gaped open.

"Hi," the young woman squeaked. "I'm Caroline, nice to meet you."

"Nice to meet you. I'm May."

She took a seat at one of the grand pianos, and I took the other. Beyond the long windows I could see oval leaves crowning a garden. There was a red couch in the corner, glowing against the whiteness of all else. Even the pianos were white.

"These are really nice." I felt the edges of the keys with my fingertips.

"Why don't you play me something so I can see where we're at?" Caroline smiled. She was almost too thin, her blonde bob accenting her sharp cheekbones. "How long have you been playing?"

"Since I was five."

Without waiting for a response, I began. *Fantasie Impromptu*, by my dear Chopin, of course. It spiraled down. Purple, purple, purple. Timid little Caroline vanished, and I sat alone with the world.

"Wow," she muttered when I finished. "That's a really hard piece. There were some rough spots, but overall that was very nice."

Rough spots. Hmm.

Secretly, I wanted her to say that I had the gift. That I was one of the best she'd ever heard. A fresh, sparkling pianist to rival the greats. That there was something in me; different, special. That I had been born for this.

Then again, she hadn't heard my own music, my creations. They were my truest talent. They were my world.

"We need to work on refining everything, just a little,"

Caroline went on, holding her finger up. Her voice was suddenly bigger. "Technically, you're fine. Musically, you're fine. But we need to push things to the next level."

I knew that boy had made it to the next level. At least artistically. I could play harder pieces, judging by his technique, but that was only half of it. There was something inside of him that I had not yet found in myself.

# Chapter Four

I really wanted to sit on the grass. Just sit on the grass, look up and count the shades of blue within.

I watched the world from my window. Everyone stepped carefully around the edges. We should stick to the pavement, I could hear them think. The dew would glue mud to their feet.

Lying on my unmade bed, I waited for time to wind away between classes. I didn't have homework, I didn't have friends, and I couldn't just run around through the fields outside. No trees, and no forest, would protect me. How far would I have to travel to find true solitude?

Those days fell upon me, upon each other, fragile yet incomprehensibly stuck. As often as I could, I escaped to the practice rooms. I didn't see that boy, though I looked.

Sometimes I imagined he was hovering in the corner behind me while I played. But I would glance over my shoulder, and no one glanced back.

Then, at my second math lecture, he was looking. The first day of class he had fallen invisible within the crowd. But not then. Not that day.

It was a concrete floor, topped by a half-circle of small desks. Faces loomed above them. So many strangers. He looked small on the other side of the room, so far away, but I knew it was him. His unhandsome features had unmistakable music in them.

His eyes felt mine. He grasped his black backpack to his chest and edged past the others in his row.

A panicked sort of embarrassment hit my stomach. I had to remind myself that I hadn't asked him to come over.

"Hi," was all he said.

"Oh, hi!" I pretended to be surprised. Pretended not to know. "You're the guy from the practice rooms, right?"

"Yeah, I'm the idiot who wouldn't let you play. Is anyone sitting there?"

I couldn't help looking at his lips while he talked. They were such a strange shape. Long and flat and dry only at the inner tip.

"Nope, go ahead."

How could he be so obvious? How could he just get up

from across the room and run to me? I may not have had a lot of boy experience, but I knew that wasn't the way guys usually acted.

At that moment the professor walked in. The whole lecture I listened, not to him, but to the boy's breathing. It was strong, purposeful. Like he consciously controlled his lungs.

Without turning my head, I looked at him; at his jeans and gray t-shirt; at his choppy brown hair.

"What was your name again?" I asked him when we stood at the end of class.

"Conner."

"I'm May," I nodded.

We walked to talk, not to get anywhere. I placed my thumbs gently in my pockets. Our talk was easy and cordial. We said the usual things. He grew up near the coast, I found out. In a town so small it only took a minute to drive through it. His dad once worked on a boat as a commercial fisherman, but had lost his job when the boat-owner died. And his mom owned a local bakery in their town. She was the provider of the family.

"I miss Venus," he said suddenly, heavily. "I haven't seen it in a few days."

"Oh." What could I have possibly said? I was silent for moment. Then, I added, "The sky is so clear here. Why haven't you seen it?"

"Hasn't been the right time. Or the right side of the sky." Conner aimed his crooked nose towards a willow branch. It rippled with the wind.

We made our way to the inner lawn, surrounded by rose bushes and thin maples. Near the cafeteria all I could smell was some sort of cake. The warmest scent imaginable.

"Look, a hawk," Conner laughed, pointing to the sloped roof of the cafeteria. Joy shined through his whole face, improving it slightly.

"Wow," I breathed. The bird was sitting right above us, leaning its beak cautiously over the edge.

Both of us stood as still as we could, watching. We were alone, at midday, eye to eye with a hawk. I had never seen one so close.

It ruffled its brown and black feathers. A tilt of the head, and then it extended its wings. Its blank eyes took some light to them. There was a tuft of feathers missing from one wing. Pumping its arms viciously, the hawk flew above us, its fluffy legs dangling below. Several feathers waded down. They landed at the very edge, straddling concrete and grass.

"A soft extension of its being." Conner bent down and whispered to the fallen plumes. Then he handed one to me.

I held it between the farthest tips of my fingers. There were specks of red and black, of almost gold. I twirled it in a circle and imagined a mountaintop. Music came into my mind. Not even a melody for piano. An entire symphony! All at once it rushed over me, behind my eyes. Following the hawk, it unraveled with the perfect tension, the perfect harmony.

"They're good luck, you know. And I don't mean the feathers." He spoke in his full voice again. "I mean the hawk."

"You're right. You're so right." I watched his eyes. Even they were not beautiful. Just dull yet glassy.

Suddenly I became aware of my own appearance. I smoothed back my eyebrows and straightened my skirt. I looked around.

Conner held his feather up to the sun. He let the light drip down his extended arm. It wove a halo around his ugliness, illuminating his silhouette. His eyes did not waver.

# Chapter Five

"Yeah, Conner's in my music theory class. He's kind of ..." Skye drew her eyes up, her long eyelashes nearly to her brow. "Well, I don't know. I guess he's pretty chill."

Our composition teacher coughed, startling our attention back to him.

"He's pretty quiet. I think he's a junior, isn't he?" Skye whispered, leaning close. She wore a long, orange hippie skirt, with her hair in a matching hue down to her waist. "And he's a music major, right?"

I nodded. It felt like I'd known Skye since high school, like she was one of my friends from home.

She was a local. The week before, she'd invited me to have dinner with her and her parents, who only lived a mile away. She had her own apartment on the other side of town, but visited them most days.

Their whole house smelled like incense; its presence sank deeply into the carpet, and onto the fluffy throw blankets. Both her parents shared Skye's same hair. Her dad's rivaled hers in length.

We ate some terrible pizza, with far too much garlic under the cheese, and watched T.V. on their old leather couch.

Then Skye played the violin. Not to show off, but because I asked her to. I picked at the stuffing leaking out of the couch while Skye played. I had to admit, she was better than Hallie. Everything sang just a little bit smoother. I felt like I was betraying my sister just for thinking it. Ranking musicians was such an opinionated thing, and shouldn't my opinion favor Hallie?

"He's kind of . . . funny looking, isn't he?" Skye bit her lip, stretching her eyes wide.

"Um . . ." It felt like another betrayal to say so aloud, though in my thoughts I had screamed it.

For some reason he was inside my mind, constantly. Not really his face, but his music; his fingers playing the Nocturne in e-flat major. I had gone back and played it myself. Much as I tried to mimic his tone, his dynamics, it wasn't the same. Not even close.

"Oh, come on. You know what I mean. You're just too nice to say so."

I pulled inward, down into my seat. Being too nice wasn't exactly a good thing. Not when there were so many other things to be. I didn't want to get stuck with any sort of reputation. Whether good or bad, I wanted none of it. Couldn't I be dynamic? Some changing, wild creature wrapped in a thousand dimensions?

After class Skye asked me to go whitewater rafting with her that weekend. I imagined us charging through water in helmets and vests, riding down the river canyon with foamy waterdrops in our eyes. Really, I wasn't the best swimmer. Nor did I know how a paddle would fit in my hand.

"No thanks." My voice rang high.

She didn't try to convince me, but let it be, as though she agreed that I was unfit for such an adventure.

The weather was still perfect and my homework was still light. I went for a walk that weekend, away from campus and to the park down the street.

It was the closest thing to a forest; a slightly higher concentration of trees than the surrounding plateau. Some of them were spacious oaks, others sparse pines. Between them there was no undergrowth. No waterleaf, or wood sorrel, or invasive ivy. Just dirt beneath the pines, and grass everywhere else.

I passed a group of fast-walking women. They were nestled in bright athletic wear, faces forward, like there was nothing around them. No beauty there. No sparrows hopping within the bushes. They were there to move their feet, and that was all.

A place like that was almost home to me. In flip-flops and shorts, I sauntered carefree throughout the park.

Something too big to be a squirrel disturbed the branch above me. Looking up, I jumped. There were human eyes between the plump acorns. A laugh came next. It was slapping and rough. I recognized it.

"Sorry." Conner swung down easily, throwing up dust when he landed. "I didn't mean to scare you."

"What were you doing up there?" I tilted my head. He had been on my mind for the entire week, yet his immediate presence annoyed me. I didn't want to see anyone. I just wanted to go for a walk.

"Just climbing. I wanted to see."

"See what?"

He took a lurching step to the side, slapping his hand against the gray trunk.

"You try it." Conner smiled with his wide front teeth.

It was an easy tree to climb, well stacked and low to the ground. I kicked off my flip-flops and gripped my toes within the cracks. With my elbows scraping the rough bark, I made it to his branch, then one higher.

Gazing out between the leaves, I expected something.

A distant river penned into the landscape. A bird's nest cradled in a neighboring tree. But there was nothing visible.

"What is it? What am I supposed to see?" I called down.

"Whatever's there." He was back on his limb.

So we sat there, in our oak tree, without counting time, without voices or words. I leaned back into the tree's heart and felt a comfort. This was right and I was a piece of the air.

"Have you found the Venus yet?" I asked after the sun wet our faces.

"No. Tell me if you see it, okay?"

"We'd better exchange phone numbers." I laughed, shifting my weight forward.

"What's yours? I don't have my phone, but I'll remember it."

"That's okay, I'll enter yours. Oh . . . I left mine in my bag down there. We can do it later."

"No, just tell me yours. I'll remember it." His eyes turned up to me, to my branch.

If I had liked him I would've smiled, and captured the moment. But I was in no danger of falling for him. As much as I hated to admit it, looks counted for something. I couldn't date someone I wasn't physically attracted to. It would be like beauty and the beast. Only, of course, that I was no true beauty, and that the beast would never resign his beastliness.

All I could do was hope he didn't get the wrong idea. Hope he didn't fall for me instead. His dim features would never burn into brilliance, not even if I wished for it.

That night he sent me a text. All it said was *told you*.

# Chapter Six

He sat at a splintering picnic bench with three girls. Judging by their smiles, they liked him, but without ease or strength. Their eyes could never rest comfortably.

If I had been him . . . how could he keep his back so straight? How did he not collapse slowly to the grass, or wander stiffly away?

One girl picked at a rusty nail with her blue-polished thumb. The other stared into a pile of papers on her lap. Only one looked at Conner as he spoke, a heavy blonde with red highlights. She watched his bent nose, then quickly flicked her gaze to the stately tree behind him.

I knew they were working on the project he'd told me about the day before. When he saw me he waved. I followed his sweeping hand and sat on the outside of the table without tucking my legs in. Crossing my ankles, I laughed with my shoulders.

"Hi," I exhaled a little too loudly.

Each of the girls positioned their mouths into round dishes, straining their necks to nod hello to me.

"Oh, um, I'm Katherine," said the blonde.

We threw around our names, until one of them sniffed and declared she had to go. They were about done, anyway. Climbing over their seats, they each escaped.

Sullenly I pivoted my legs through the empty space, chaining myself within the bench. My bare thighs felt the bristles of peeling wood. They itched to spin the other way.

Conner sorted through his folder, coughing emptily. In the sunlight his hair was tarnished to a muddy gray. From the side, his visage jutted out into a crude lump. There was nothing outwardly distinct about him. If any shape at all he was a blob.

"I'm learning 'Pathetique'." He tucked his folder into his backpack.

"Wow." Beethoven's sonatas aren't easy.

"I think that's one I'll play for the panel." He stood, knocking his knees into the tabletop.

Once per term we had to play in front of the judges. We were assigned to pick something from each era; Baroque, Classical, Romantic, and Modern.

Our grades came from the judges' ears. From how strong we held a bridge along our knuckles.

I had played in front of judges before, to test what level I was at. Having them there didn't make me any more nervous. Not even the ones who only swallowed and offered a brief thank-you. They were just listening. That was all.

"Caroline wants me to wait on *Fantasie Impromptu* until next term. Maybe I'll do some Beethoven, too." I slid down to the edge of the bench and rose. "Maybe one of his sonatas?"

"A different one, please," he laughed.

Both of us were standing, our backs to the tree's shadow. He opened his mouth and then didn't say anything.

"What are you doing this weekend?" I hung my thumbs from my pockets.

"I don't know exactly." Conner paused, his flat eyes seeking the source of a bird's call. "There's this girl in one of my classes."

Oh no.

"I really like her." His eyebrows crushed together.

Of course he meant me. Why did he have to do this?

"You might know her, actually . . ."

Please don't.

"I think you guys are friends. Skye? She's in my composition class."

My chest remained tight. Nodding, I pushed a little laugh from my throat.

"I can't tell if she likes me or not."

Good, I wanted to say, but within his stretching tone of voice I could hear hope. Where had it come from? Where had it possibly come from?

His mouth serious, Conner shrugged.

"I'll just have to ask her to come on a hike with me."

I didn't ask why because my cheeks were already hot. Within them I felt a beaming shame that I had no words for.

"Right," I said.

Conner's hands clenched, then unfurled. A western scrub jay landed on the table. It had eyes like a robin, but a flat, twisting body like any other jay. Joyfully, it left crooked tracks along the dusty wood.

"They are more than just mountains to him," Conner hummed, "that separate us from the sea."

"What's that from?" I watched the bird scrape its beak into the cracks.

He took his eyes from the scrub jay and shook his head.

"Did you know that steller's jays can mimic other birds? Sometimes they even try to sound like a red-tailed hawk . . ."

"This is a scrub jay." I set down my bag. "See, it doesn't have a crest."

"Yes. It is. It just *reminded* me of the steller's jay."

His hair kept blowing in his eyes but he didn't move it. Instead he blinked and blinked, wrinkling up his forehead. Every so often he looked far across the fields, as though there was something he wanted to run to.

"You know the forests at the edge of the hills?" Conner asked, standing still with his knees locked.

"Yeah." I had often pointed my chin in their direction. They were beyond the meadows swept up in dry grasses, beyond the low peaks that plunged gently upward into hills. From their summits you could reach for the mountain's face. Creeks braided their feet together, where little patches of pines marched steadily across the skyline.

I longed to inch along the eternal forest's yellow light. To taste the muddy wind. To sweep my hand above the rows of ferns, mimicking the water I could only hear. It would be just behind those blackberry thorns, hiding . . . show me, little finches, hop your way there . . .

"Do you think Skye would be into that? Going for a hike up that way?"

"Hell yeah. I would totally be into that." There was Skye behind us, her straight white teeth on display. Ignoring the sun, her neck was wrapped in a patterned scarf. She swung her braided hair off her shoulder. "Wait . . . seriously, you guys are talking about me?"

With Skye's laugh the bird darted to the tree at our backs. Tilting around, I watched it jump between branches. It didn't even move its wings.

"Are you coming?" Skye turned to me.

"Me? No, I've got homework."

Conner didn't mouth *thank you*, but I knew he wanted to.

Poor Conner. He would eventually find out what Skye thought of him.

As the bird fanned its blue feathers over us, I remembered, suddenly, that scrub jays don't usually live so far east.

# Chapter Seven

They weren't smoking yet, but they'd invited me to join them at the park later.

"If I have time."

The answer, really, was *hell no*. I knew I would go back to my little studio and sit on the bed again. Unless smoking could somehow inspire me to create stronger music, there was just no reason. No reason to risk the trouble.

One of Skye's friends hid the weed in her pocket. A braided, purple headband rested above her weak eyebrows. We walked in a pack of five. Me, Skye, Headband Girl, a boy with drooping holes in his ears, and another girl. Her jeans were rolled up to her pale calves, revealing wool socks tucked into sandals.

"Ugh, it was terrible. He walked *so slow*, and he kept stopping to look at things. I mean, it wasn't even a hike, you know? I could've walked the trail twice in the time it took him to walk half of it."

"And I thought he'd be all outdoorsy," Sandal Girl snorted. She rubbed one snake of hair, half-dreaded with a brown feather at its root.

"All he wore were just some crappy sneakers, and it was, like, pretty steep."

"Why'd you agree to go out with him?" the Boy stiffly asked, each word a distinct punch.

"I didn't. I just wanted to go for a hike and he was a free ride. He's an ugly little shit, anyway."

We laughed collectively at her outrageousness. My eyes bent toward the pavement, and stayed still for a little too long. I crossed my arms.

"So do you want to come?" Skye drew in her lips to stop laughing.

"No, that's okay. I've got some stuff to do, anyway." I wrinkled one cheek and leaned to the left. The path to my apartment was there.

"Well at least come to the party tomorrow night. It's at Turner's place." She winked. It was a real wink. Only her eyelid moved.

The group headed off toward the park, waving from the side, their faces turned from me. I walked the steps without feeling them beneath me.

When I turned on the light, my clutter revealed itself. I didn't want a place for everything; it seemed to me their place could be everywhere. The room needed to breath.

There were books in towering stacks on the floor, and blankets in thick piles at the bed's ankles. The bathroom counter was cluttered with mascara and eye shadow, but my clothes were tucked into the dresser, and my dishes were clean. The sink was always empty, anyway.

One window was open, so the whole room smelled like night. I opened my laptop onto the fold-out kitchen table. While it loaded, I grabbed an orange from the fridge. Its juice made my tongue coil.

Something drew me to Facebook. Suddenly I was typing in Conner's name, but nothing came up. Either he had strict privacy settings, or he had resisted the cultural Facebook urge.

My shoulders ached. Stretching my arms up, I sighed. I'd wanted to see what his profile picture looked like. Would he smile like he had convinced himself he was handsome?

Part of me felt like I should be at the park. Like I should crave acceptance and care a little more. Like I should've at least stood there with them, even if I didn't smoke. I should have stood there with my hands in my pockets, and my face dry and unimpressed.

Next time I would inhale the wind and *stand there,* just so they'd remember my presence.

There was no music in that; in blankness and stretched smiles. Still, I needed friends. I would go to the party, I decided. Of course I would.

I spent the next morning trying to write out a piece. My hand scribbled the circles and spines, but it wasn't quite right. It was a melody devoid of satisfaction. Maybe it was because I was trying too hard, hunched over the table with my fingers clutching my scalp.

Instead I showered. Then I rubbed black liner under my eyes, watching my mirror glitter through the fogginess. I forced myself to sip coffee choked with sugar.

Nothing more came, so I tried humming. I let sound escape my throat until it shuddered in gritty protest.

The afternoon came and I had done nothing more than stare at the window. Not out it, but at the glass itself. It was green along the edges, in a subtle, brown way. There were smudges toward the bottom where my thumbs had pushed it up. This was my place. My own territory.

It seemed like it would hurt to change my clothes, or to cover my face in colors far more beautiful than I could naturally effervesce. My greatest obligation of the night was to look unlike myself.

So I chose a short dress that zippered up the front, and wedges. I straightened my hair, then loosely curled the pieces that framed my cheeks. The lighting in the bathroom made my makeup look caked on, like it was balled up and made of sand. After checking in the hallway's lighting with a compact mirror, I decided I had on just enough.

"May!" The voice came before the knock.

As I opened the door, Skye's earthy vanilla perfume flowed in. Her nose was pointed toward her phone.

"Hey." I ran my tongue along my teeth.

"Hey, you look cute," she said quietly, slapping her phone into her pocket. "Ready to go?"

Skye's jaw moved as she chewed her gum. A car wove through the street behind her, washing the pavement with red light. The air moaned. For some reason the sky was densely clouded, and it, too, burned a dusty red.

We descended the wooden stairs more carefully than we needed to. Skye looked pale in the darkness. Her black tank and leather skirt worked harsh lines against her full limbs. She was curvy in a way that made her neck look athletic, but her ankles skinny.

"Where are we going, again?" I puffed my voice out because we had started walking faster.

"It's at Turner's. You don't know him, but you'll know some of the other people. Evan's the one who got us in."

I nodded, but Skye was picking something off her shirt, so she didn't see. She seemed tired. Or maybe just contemplative.

"Mmhmm," I murmured. I thought of the parties I'd gone to in high school. We sat around, ate chips, and talked. Or, if we were feeling really daring, we sang crying mumbles into Ashley's karaoke machine before choking with laughter.

The neighborhoods lining the campus were muffled behind blinds. All of their cars were in their driveways, and their porch lights were turned off. I followed Skye down the sleeping side streets. A car drove past us, then another, until we came to the house all the cars were driving to.

A pulse of sound, not music, shook the walls. It vibrated along the line of parked cars, along the clustered bodies holding cups. We became a mass of pounding noise.

Inside, the small house looked dim but not threatening. I wiped my palm on the side of my dress, just in case anyone Skye introduced me to was a hand-shaker.

"Evan!" Skye yelled, her voice approaching a quavering squeak. In two steps they were hugging so closely that her forehead rested on his inner shoulder. He lifted one thin arm, but she was still pressed against him. It was as though he had poured life into her breathing lungs, scooped her in, and stolen the spark once again.

Evan's dark eyes squinted at me. His eyelashes and brows were so pale I thought he had none. Maybe he had lost them through some terrible disease. I could imagine him crying over the sink as lashes waded down, the tears capturing even more of them. Then he turned his neck to nod to someone behind, and there was their weak shadow, after all.

How did such paleness breed chocolate eyes? It was as though he was an evil god, and those eyes his power. Their frame was robust. Like someone who claims to be a mountain climber, the greatest there ever was, but has really never set foot beyond the valley . . .

I clumped my hair to one side with my empty hands, then tossed it back behind me. Finally, Skye stepped away from him.

"Sammy brought a shit-load of beer." Evan opened his mouth into some sort of a fake scream. "It's in a cooler next to the table."

"Nice." Skye dove through the thin, crowded hallway toward it. I followed along behind her.

The floors were old yellow tile. Something from a grandmotherly kitchen that enveloped the entire house. Alongside the plain walls, it made the place look broken. That was not the floor for a party; not for gasping to the lyrics I knew nothing of, nor making out in the corner so everyone could just see through the muted light. It looked better for making tea. There were dark circles and dashes on it. What color, I couldn't quite tell.

I was caught in the pattern until we entered the room with the stereo. The thumping stirred me from my trance. On the wall was a poster of Bob Marley, framed and hung perfectly straight. There was no other furniture, no decorations. Just people.

"Are you drunk already?" Evan swung his hands over his head. Skye was rocking her hips back and forth.

"No." She threw him a savage glance, then shyly smiled. "But this isn't my first beer."

She held up her plastic cup with a tilted wrist. For the first time I noticed the dilution to her voice. I approached the plastic cooler timidly, my ears burning as I unlatched a can and poured it into a cup.

When I looked back at Skye and Evan, the girl with the sandals had joined them. I had never seen her wear anything but Birkenstocks.

"Hey!" I stood in their circle. The three only nodded in response, offbeat with the music. I held the plastic cup with both hands and locked it between my lips. A biting stench emerged, but I sipped it anyway. I could feel its whole, spiraling journey down my throat. Much as I hated it, it seemed the right thing to do.

"Arianna," Evan whispered, but I could still follow his lips. "The whole galaxy is on your ass."

"What the hell?" She half-stomped one of her sandaled

feet. "Skye, did you hear what he said to me?"

Biting the rim of her cup, she turned in a circle, her hands on her hips while she eyed the back of her shorts.

"He thinks I have a fat ass."

"Holy shit, don't overreact. It looks good," Evan laughed.

I considered what we would've looked like a hundred years before. If we had been partygoers in the late Romantic era. Would we not have gowns to our ankles, our hair done up in proprietous buns? Evan would bow to us in his freshly pressed suit. His eyebrows would certainly be penciled in to a darker hue.

And surely I would've sat down at the piano as they all gathered around to listen and to marvel at my talent; all with good posture and their gloved hands placed just so on the rim. Then we would eat sweet little pastries while discussing art, literature, music. In a world like that, I would never be obscure.

"May! Dance with me!" Skye shrieked. A new song had begun its hammering. Some guy with dreadlocks and a neck tattoo took up the offer instead, entering the throbbing, sweating rhythm of the others. As I stepped closer I realized the tattoo was a ruby-throated hummingbird.

I felt suddenly covered in glue. Clutching the cup against my opposite armpit, I pushed my way to the front door as discretely as I could. Then I stopped. Even through the tiny window I recognized rain. I knew how to look slanted through the air, how to catch the transparent drops in the side of the light. Sighing, I twisted back around.

Dripping the last of the beer down my throat, I stood again next to Skye. From the shadowy corner emerged a boy hardly taller than me, a bit chubby in the face. He slipped behind me. His wet hands found my waist.

"Want to dance?" he blew in my ear. It smelled somewhere between sick and alcohol.

"I'm going to get more beer." I rushed away, my head squarely, embarrassingly forward.

But once more from the shadows came a boy, this one with built arms falling from a white tank top. His face spared no wrinkles as it moved, as though it were plastic. From lips too pink for his olive skin, he spoke.

"I'm Eugene."

I would've laughed at his name if his voice hadn't been quite so steady. He wrapped his thumbs, warm but arid, around my wrists. My empty cup sank soundlessly to the tile floor. Pulling me gently toward him, he positioned my hands on the crevice between his neck and shoulders.

"What's your major?" he asked me, not loudly, but closely.

"Music. Piano," I breathed. We were swaying together,

a slow-dance despite how the song raced frantically through inorganic tones. I hoped dearly that my underarms weren't sweaty enough to show.

Then he leaned in and he kissed me. Right there, my wedges glued with dry beer to the grandma tiles, surrounded by groping, heated strangers. On his tongue I could taste what I hadn't smelled before.

"Your lips are chapped," I told him, but he seemed not to hear. All he did was stand there with his red-veined eyes half closed.

Stomping clumsily toward the front door, I kept my head down. Then I turned the plastic doorknob, pressed the door against the crowd, and swung myself out. The rain hit my hair, wild and caressed by wind. All the other houses along the street were dark. How could they even pretend to sleep? I sat down on the curb, dirty rain soaking immediately through my dress. Instinctively I wanted to turn my face away so my makeup wouldn't be dented. But it didn't matter anymore.

I was supposed to be there, wasn't I? Partying, socializing, looking for boys? I'd had a beer and been seen. Maybe that was success enough. So what if my second kiss, like my first, had been stolen? I was an artist, a composer, and knew such an experience could produce beauty.

The rain was colder than it had ever felt at home. It was

a different sort; short and slicing. In the corner of the sky a cloud thinned, and white moonlight showed dully through. Although it was masked, the moon carried me into it, up to it. I whispered a mental hello, watching breathlessly until brown clouds once again stifled its glow.

# Chapter Eight

"Hey, girl, you ready to go?" Skye was behind me, the loop of her tank top slung loosely over her shoulder.

I didn't rise from the curb until her foot grazed my thigh.

"Skye, I've been waiting for you for like *five hours*. I couldn't walk home by myself in the dark, so I was kind of stuck here. Waiting for you."

"Well how was I 'sposed to know you were sitting out here by yourself? You shoulda come in and danced, right?" Her voice was thick with dew.

There was nothing for me to say. My skin was itchy and old, my throat coated in sourness. Everything but the robin's morning songs seemed distant. When I allowed myself to look at Skye I found her almost unchanged from the night before. Her hair had fuzzed near her forehead, and her dark eye liner was blotchy, but otherwise she held her usual bohemian charm.

"Oh my god . . . what the- what- wha- where's my bracelet?" Skye gasped. She hopped up and down, half sleepy, half energetic.

"Were you ever even *wearing* a bracelet?" I started walking away from the party house. It was light. I could walk back on my own if I had to.

Skye followed me, swearing and panting at the warm morning air. We passed by blonde fathers holding garden hoses, robed grandmothers on their porches. They subtly shook their heads and tilted their lips up in secret smiles. Our short skirts obviously clashed with the newly born sky.

We parted without words. In my apartment, tired tears drowned my sight. Suddenly I missed my parents. I didn't want to tell them what happened. I just wanted to talk to them. When I called they didn't answer. Too early. They probably thought it was a sales call. I imagined them hardly opening their eyes and letting it ring.

For a moment I stood in the middle of the room. I hovered there and locked my knees until I felt faint. Swallowing dry washes of air, I fell to my bed. I realized I was past the point where sleep could come easily, but my mind was far too numb to do anything besides lay and stare.

My phone was on the pillow next to me, and I sat it on my chest. I texted Conner: *You must be jealous. I saw Venus.*

His reply came so quickly I thought for a second he'd initiated the conversation, and our messages had only crossed paths. Then I read the response. *You would be wrong. I'm not jealous because I saw it too.*

I threw my phone back down onto the pillow and entombed it under another. Finally I rested my cheek, shut my sore eyelids, and fell asleep.

The sun was cutting through the blinds. My phone told me, in clean, black letters, that it was three in the afternoon. I had left my window open a crack the whole time we were gone, and I could still smell the way the rain had hit the walls.

If I didn't move around and do something I felt like I would never forgive myself. Like I would be trapped forever in some sort of box.

Soon I was dressed and walking to the practice rooms, a stack of music books under my arm. Skye had texted me that she was *so hungover*. I replied that I was too, although I didn't mean it in the same way she did. The party was stuck to me. I wanted it off.

Sundays were the least busy days in the practice rooms. My footsteps were vacant and spongy over the carpet, echoing even without the aid of tile. In my solitude I twirled freely into a glass box. I dropped my books at the piano's side, then shut the door. Biting my lip, I opened it again, just a sliver of myself exposed. For air, I told myself. Of course, what I really wanted was for someone to hear me.

First I did scales, then some finger strengthening exercises. It was the best piano, a rich old grand that reminded me of my own. Something struck me, and I began to play without a key, without a direction, without thinking at all. At first it was peaceful, then tense. Like laying on your belly at the top of a tower, all the ocean rolled out in front of you. Then you see the trees shudder. The very same wind hits you next; burning, sodden. You just cry and cry and wipe your eye on your sleeve, because you know you have to leave, and when you look down you see that, really, there was never a tower at all. You have been falling this whole time. Falling and falling and . . .

I could feel them looking at my back. They passed on and said nothing, but they'd heard it all.

Closing my eyes, I continued playing.

You have to have something, something to carry with you always; to guide you and calm you and nourish you. If I didn't have piano, I would've had nothing. My days would've been so empty that I would have stopped waking up at all, hiding myself instead in some sullen corner of the world.

Concentrating on my fingers was all that kept me from sobbing. What was so confusing, what was all torn up in my chest? Why was it that other people made me feel so unbearably small?

I left the piano without closing its cover, suddenly hungry. The sky was already drifting away. Above the hills ran a cool, white cloak anticipating the darkness to come. I walked underneath a row of small maples, standing on my toes to stroke their blossoming, orange-traced leaves. They quivered but refused to fall. I reached up my other hand, too, and let their corners tickle me. The helicopters were brown and mostly fallen.

When I was little I used to climb the orchard trees, carefully pinching the flat, hairless end of the maple seed. Nothing near the maple trees was climbable, so I would sculpt a pile of helicopters at the base of one apple tree or another. Then I would toss a helicopter out in front of me. Slipping and spiraling through the air, it caught the currents like a heedless bird.

"The squirrels love samaras," a pinched voice said.

I threw my hands down at my sides and pretended I'd only been stretching, rather than stroking the leaves. Clutching them together in front of my stomach, I turned to Conner.

"Samaras?"

"The little helicopters." He pointed to one of the v-shaped seeds, still green. "The squirrels eat them. They like the bark on the maple trees, too."

"I've seen them, they scrape it off branches with their teeth." I remembered discovering pale ribbons on the soil, remnants of the squirrel's feasting.

There was a moment of silence, but Conner seemed unafraid of it. He smiled crudely up at the tree. As always he was wearing a plain t-shirt, unadorned and unassuming, with Teva sandals on his feet.

"Why do I always run into you everywhere?" I laughed in a snorty way through my nose.

He widened his sagging eyes.

"Where were you headed?" I asked quickly.

"Nowhere." He said it like it was obvious. Like it was the most exciting thing in the world.

"Oh. I was just going to go get something to eat."

"That sounds good. I'll join you," Conner paused, staring pensively at what felt like the space between my eyes. "If that's okay."

"Oh, yeah, sure," I nodded. Even though I wanted desperately to be alone, there was no way I could refuse without sounding rude.

We followed the path, quietly studying the cracks it held. His walk was heavy and drifting, indecisive like his build. I decided not to try. It was only Conner, after all. If he asked me how my weekend went, I would make a quick excuse and slip away. But he didn't.

Our cafeteria was old like the rest of the university, though not in quite as regal a way. It was a cave of dark wood panels, fragrant with a thousand things fried at once. The food was surprisingly decent; a buffet, a sandwich bar, soups, and the daily special on display right at the front.

Conner scooped out a salad. I chose the special—spaghetti shining in a yellow grease of olive oil. I was neither across from him nor next to him at the round table, so when I glanced up from my plate I could avoid looking at him directly.

"I want to hear you one of these days." He licked a green fleck off his lower lip.

"Yeah?" I sniffed, still chewing.

"I bet you're really good."

I did think I was good. Truthfully, immodestly, good. But how could I tell him that?

"Well." I glanced at the ceiling, crossing my arms over the clammy plastic tabletop. "I don't know . . ."

"Yeah, you're good. You must be." He lifted his shoulders to straighten his posture. "Why didn't you go to Julliard or anything?"

"Money." I stopped my fork mid-bite and shrugged.

"There's no way I could've gone anywhere out of state, even with a scholarship."

"Hmm. Yeah," Conner laughed, a gritty chuckle that rose from his gut. "You're definitely good, then."

"Why . . ."

"You automatically assume you would've gotten in. *And* gotten a scholarship."

I took in a breath and left it there, unsure whether to laugh.

"It's not like I didn't apply."

His face had been peripheral to mine until that moment. I carefully sent my eyes toward his bumped and shadowy expression. Conner just squinted.

"We couldn't pay," I continued, "and they didn't want me enough to offer me what I needed."

"But you got in."

"I got in." Saying it aloud was painful. I had ignored the piano for a week when I found out. My only chance at a big enough scholarship was gone, and without it I was trapped. I was trapped in a place that could never make me immortal.

Only my parents knew I had applied. And Hallie. She told me they were all stuck-up at Julliard, anyway. All the out-of-state schools I applied to were full of rich, passionless brats. I told myself that, too. I hated them after that. Those snobby, heartless robots.

"It doesn't really matter where you go to school, anyway. Just what you do *after*," he told me.

But without the opportunities of a prestigious school, I would never study in Europe, or make the right connections, or do *anything* . . .

"It's all just for playing, right?" Conner continued softly. "You can do that anywhere."

"You're right." I didn't ask him why *he* hadn't gone to Julliard. The familiarity of his words, the sad twitch to his blinking . . . he knew firsthand what I had been through. He had known the pain of failure. There was nothing we could do about the money, but maybe, maybe if we had been *better* a passage would've opened for us.

Or maybe Conner knew pain because he saw it every time someone looked at him.

"Ready?" I asked. Our plates were stained and empty.

He only grunted in an affirmative sort of way, so we stood and crept from one darkness to another.

"There's Jupiter." He motioned with all his fingers at once.

I saw its wide, circular beam behind the clear air. It pulled on us in a steady yellow dance.

"You know what that means," he said.

"What?"

We wandered in front of the cafeteria with our necks bent and our eyes content to scrape the heavens. Nothing could make the earth beneath us any sweeter than what we saw in the skies.

"It's going to be winter soon," he said.

"Oh no!"

"Oh *no*? There's nothing wrong with winter," his voice drifted off. "It's just as good as all the other seasons."

Beneath the stars, everything was grand and playful. I wanted to roll and leap in a big field. We were always in a sort of field; the horizon carved its own meadow wherever it went.

"Look at the stars. The moon's not up yet, and look how bright they are." I smiled until I could no longer see, until my cheeks rolled up under my ears. Why had it been so long since I'd last sat with the stars?

Who was missing this? Who was inside, or in a car, or in another place? The world never seemed truer than when I was looking *outside* of it, and into the eyes of the universe. I realized I had been without it for too long. I mouthed some exclamatory nonsense, just so I could feel a word on my lips.

A little ways out from the buildings and their lights, the two of us laid down on the grass to watch the sky. I couldn't smell the grass itself, despite my hair spilling over the crunching, feathered field. There was wind above us as we sank slowly into last night's rain.

"There's Lyra. And Hercules." I ran my fingers over the constellations. "Oh! And Bootes."

"What's your favorite constellation?" Conner asked, his nose parallel to the stripes of the sky. He wasn't at all surprised that, like him, I knew the stars.

"Orion, I guess. In the winter."

"See. Winter never deserved your contempt." He strained his neck, bringing it up from the earth, then eased back down.

# Chapter Nine

I wasn't quite sure what it meant, but he invited me on a hike, and I wanted to go. Conner had his own car, a dark yellow thing with stiff seats, old enough that I didn't even know what kind it was. We sat in near silence the whole way over to the hills. Despite its age, his car smelled only like some un-placeable herb.

At my feet was a topographic map ripped in two. In the back, an empty aluminum water bottle rolled. It rang against the seats each time he accelerated, but he let it. So did I. In a hollow way it was enchanting, accompanying the sweeping landscape so gently.

The only way I could look was out the window. Conner's face was cut up by the sun, all blemished and swollen. He gripped the steering wheel without any force, but watched the road intently.

"So," I tried. "Have you been here before? Where we're going?"

"No. I don't even know where we're going." His voice was small and confined within the car.

"What?" I laughed, glancing at him.

"Let's pick a spot and just go." He lifted one hand and threw it up.

"Sure. As long as we don't get lost."

"We won't."

Pines built up around us. Within them I saw a stream, and the sun fluttering on the rocks beneath it.

"There," I said. "Let's stop there."

Conner pulled over to a ditch. He shoved open the door with his shoulder, dropped the keys in the pocket of his shorts, and stood looking at the ground. I threw on my backpack and followed him.

"Are we allowed to park here?"

"Why not?"

The dusty asphalt burned quietly with mid-morning steam. I listened to my breath, to the birds and to the silence of the forest, to the water within it. I began to feel the heaviness of our distance from civilization.

Despite his deep, grainy voice and his hardy shape, Conner seemed just a boy in front of me. This was not my backyard. This was not a planned, weekend camping trip.

This was a random block of wilderness neither of us knew. There were no paths drawn for us, no ranger station to call for help. No one even knew where we were. Of course they didn't; we didn't even know where we were.

I felt suddenly attached to the road, unwilling to leave it behind. There was nature and then there was wilderness. I hadn't asked for the latter.

"Will we make it back before it gets dark out?" I tried to keep my voice flat.

"I don't know." Conner looked at the handle on the car door, then at me.

"Do you need a map or something?"

"No."

"Well what if we get lost?"

"You're the one who wanted to stop here. If we get lost we'll be fine. It's warm and there's still a ton to eat." He slipped his hands in his pockets.

"Well maybe if we just go in and look at the creek, and come back and drive to a better spot? Like where there's a trail or something?"

Conner nodded as he walked beneath the shoulders of the pines. The sun was left alone where it had clutched his head.

I stepped onto the pillow of fallen, orange needles. They weren't as fragrant as I thought they would be, and instead

I smelled only mud. That smell seemed to wrap around my head, into my ears, up my nostrils. It swaddled me in a muffled tarp I couldn't shake away. This was the muddy wind I had wished for, but it tasted foreign and ominous.

As I trudged toward the glistening boulders rising smoothly from the stream, Conner leaped out of sight. The next moment he was crouched beside the water. He stuck his fingers in. That was when I noticed his feet—all he wore were sandals.

"Conner," I said. I continued sidling down the incline toward him. "What's up with your shoes?"

"What?"

"It's mid-October. We're in the forest."

"It's still warm out."

"Yeah, but what if you step on something, or something?" I glanced down at my own hiking boots, stuffed with wool socks. "How can you really hike in those? Especially off-trail?"

He pushed into the dry earth and jumped up. A woodpecker laughed, its call reaching down the cracked trunks of the Ponderosa Pines.

"I don't hike like you do. I just . . . walk."

"How do you know how I hike?" I exhaled, finally reaching the creek bed.

Conner smiled. One side of his mouth stretched higher

than the other. He laughed a little through his mountainous nose. I clenched my teeth and stared at a wild tuft of grass.

I had only taken a few steps, what did *he* know? How could he assume so much already? I was a forest girl, but this was the wrong side of the mountain. It was more open, less lush. Besides, I had never hiked much. I had just . . . played, or sat beneath the trees.

Part of me wanted to sit on the hood of the car and demand Conner drive me home. I crossed the creek in a swift dance over the rocks, arriving on the other side with dry feet. Conner waded through.

We continued on, past some flowering bushes I had no name for. Next to a spindly Larch was a Madrone tree. I recognized its peeling, clay-colored bark.

"Huh. Didn't think they grew in this area." He reached into its low branches and pulled out a pink, grape-like berry. He dropped it on his tongue.

I'd heard they were edible, but I had never tried one. Before he finished chewing, I had a rubbery Madrone berry in my own mouth.

"Doesn't taste like much," I said as I shoved it to the side of my cheek.

"Tastes like Madrone to me."

We kept walking. Conner both shrunk into the forest and stood above it. He was so calm and so woven into the landscape that it seemed he was a tree himself. Every so often he glanced down, around, up.

The road had dissolved behind us, as had the creek.

"Do you ever compose?" Conner asked. He crept along in soft footsteps, watching me over his shoulder.

"How did you know?"

"You have it. I can tell." His smile pushed up the creases in his forehead.

Poor Conner. He wasn't quite ugly enough to be pitied for disfigurement, or to be gawked at, yet it was hard to ignore. It wasn't so much his ugliness that bothered me. It was how I felt for unwillingly noticing it. If he had been good-looking, even just average-looking, the pain in my side would've disappeared.

"You've got something in your head right now, don't you," he said.

"I always do."

It was true, but there were other things in my head besides compositions. I wondered what he thought of me. Maybe I was ugly to him. Maybe he thought we were a perfect, unsightly match, fit to hide away together in the woods. Beauty is subjective, after all.

"Who's your favorite composer?" He gripped the stem of a vine maple.

"Chopin," I said with a nod.

Conner's lip stretched into that same half-smile.

"I thought for sure you were going to say Mozart or Haydn."

"I like their symphonies, but Chopin's my favorite composer for piano." I paused. "What about you?"

"I could never really decide. Maybe Liszt. He's my favorite to play."

"Liszt? You have to have really big hands to play Liszt."

"Yep." He raised his palm and wiggled his fingers. "Have—" He froze, staring intently at an exposed cluster of roots.

Calm yellow eyes stared back. A bobcat slipped out from behind the tree, bounding in front of us on wide, fluffy paws. I tried not to breath. Its ears were tipped with black tufts; strings, like candle wicks. Each ear flicked, and then its stubby tail faced us. It reminded me of a human on all fours, the way its back legs were longer than its front legs. Twigs snapped beneath it as it ran from us.

I felt like I should say something, anything.

"Have you ever seen a bobcat before?" I asked, because Conner kept staring and staring with his head bent in awed reverence.

"Haven't *you*?" asked Conner gruffly.

"Not that close."

"Wonder what he's doing out so early. Anyway, don't worry, they don't go after people."

"I know. But there's still something in those eyes. Makes you want to jump back."

We walked on, past branches crusty with dry moss. Past thin, white leaf skeletons dangling from spider webs. The sun was our guide, but we followed it carelessly. There was always something to kneel down and caress, or to gape at with our heads tilted back.

I began to feel the same steadiness I had known in my own forest. Each step farther from the road and the car and the college, the deeper the fullness crept into my chest. I wanted to hum, and I knew Conner wouldn't mind, but I couldn't. Not next to him. Only the trees should hear.

His face would have looked blank to anyone else, but I could tell something profound lurked behind his grave eyes. He would unravel the universe, I thought, or at least bring us closer to the parts of it we couldn't see.

My feet grew hot and my legs grew tired, so we sat at the base of a pine tree. Half the day had passed. I looked at my phone, but I was far enough out of service that it wouldn't even show the time. I sorted through my backpack until I found the Clif bar shoved at the bottom.

"I brought some snacks," I said as I tore open the wrapper. "Do you want anything?"

"No thanks."

Without ever truly standing, he reached toward a nearby tree trunk. Nestled beneath it was a row of tiny green plants. They looked soft and crisp, each topped by a flat rectangle almost like butterfly wings. Conner plucked one by its stem, then another, until he had a handful. Then he stuffed all of them in his mouth.

"Conner, I have food. You don't have to eat *that*."

"Haven't you ever tried miner's lettuce?"

Before he finished speaking, I was chewing the watery plant. It really did taste almost like lettuce.

White flowers crowned their tips, so small I hadn't noticed them before. Each point was like a colorless brushstroke of sunlight.

"When we eat from the forest, it grows inside us," he said.

Conner leaned back into his tree, and I into mine. The wind broke over us, warm but haunted by nightfall. I knew we should be heading back, but I didn't want to leave, and I didn't want Conner to think I did.

"Shouldn't we start back pretty soon?" I asked, crushing my voice into a low murmur.

"If we do we'll be walking in the dark," he answered smoothly. "We're at least eight miles from the road and the sun's almost down."

I stood, stumbling, and inhaled sharply.

"What does that mean?"

"It means we're staying here tonight," Conner said. His calm smile was more hideous than ever.

# Chapter Ten

Couldn't we run? Couldn't we bolt to the car and chase the darkness away? Couldn't we climb a tree to find cell service, and call for help? Or even brave the darkness and use my phone's screen as a guiding light?

A night in the wilderness . . . and it was getting so much colder. What if we were lost forever? Did we really even know which direction led to the road?

What if . . . what if we died? Suddenly I was famished and thirsting to death. I couldn't hold on to my backpack without dropping it. What if we were attacked? No one would know where to find us.

What if the sun never came up?

I stood with my arms crossed, touching my knuckles to my lip every so often. Conner arranged sticks on the ground.

With a pile of larger branches at his side, he stacked twigs
and moss in a triangle. He pulled a flint fire-starter from
his pocket and aimed it at the fluffy crescent of moss. With
one strike the dry bundle was eaten by the spark. He blew
into it and dropped it swiftly beneath the dome of wood.
The flame licked away gently, without any urgency at all.

"I'm fine with sleeping out here," Conner said, "but if
you want a shelter I'll help you build one."

That made me want to cry, although I couldn't say why
exactly. I pushed my eyebrows together and stared at the
dirt. The trees were already turning gray.

"Okay. Yeah. I used to make forts when I was little."

We stabbed a strong, branching stick into the dust, and
leaned a longer stick against it diagonal to the ground. Along
its side we draped smaller branches, dead leaves, and ferns.
Only a little hole was left open in the front. I crawled inside
and laid more ferns on the floor. The shelter was tight,
warm, and surprisingly sturdy. My hands stopped shaking.

"What do we do now?" I asked. I couldn't stop blinking.
All I wanted was to be home, really home, with my parents.

"Don't worry."

"How can I not, we're *lost*—"

"No we're not." He sat next to his fire in the powdery
dirt, his legs crossed tightly underneath him. His hair
looked longer than usual as the sunset stole its clarity, and
his chin disappeared into his neck.

"Well what are we, then?" My voice shrank away.

"We're late and we're camping out, that's all."

That's all. That wasn't all. I had a music history paper to write when I got back, I had practicing to do. I was hungry and my calves were tight from walking.

Conner stared pensively into the fire. He pushed out his ugly, choppy lips and breathed in the red smoke.

"You may be used to all of this, but I'm not," I said. "And I know you planned it."

His eyes were rimmed with tiredness. He gazed at me with less surprise than I'd expected.

"What did I plan?"

"Never mind. I just want to go home."

"Tomorrow," he spit.

I sat across from him so the flame would hide his face. The night came quietly. Light pulled away from the branches, leaving them matte and naked and alone. Then daylight receded, drifting further into the mysterious sky. We could see only glimpses of it, waning and free of clouds.

Finally, when it seemed hopelessly dead, the sun tore through once more. Its frail arms stroked the earth through whatever holes the tree-shadows could bear. But it lasted for only a moment. The winds changed direction and the birds gave their last whistles. The invisible air turned still and dark.

Only the pines grew more intimidating at night. Everything else shriveled away, lying low enough to look up at the spotted undersides of the ferns.

A woodpecker tapped fearlessly behind us. *Tick-tick-tick* echoed at the final blast of dusk, and that was the last noise. The fire popped and curled, but it couldn't begin to cover up the silence.

There was the mimicking starlight of Jupiter. It surfaced over the lacy line that the trees wove between themselves; their own copy of the horizon. It was late, but my stomach hurt and I knew I wouldn't sleep. My hands felt dirty. I wanted to wash my face or at least tie my hair back into a ponytail.

"It's only one night," Conner said.

"Yeah." My friendliness toward him was to end right there. I was determined never to see him again if we ever returned to school. It was his fault that my bare arms were beginning to ache with cold. "And I hate you for it."

"What, was I walking alone?" His skin was orange. I could only see his eyes when he turned his face to the side and the fire shined off of them.

"Might as well have been."

"You led us here. You wanted to stop by the creek, you wanted to walk this way. You lost track of time."

"So did you," I said with my teeth clenched.

"But it doesn't bother me. We're meant to be here."

"*Meant* to be here? Oh my god. Look at you. You hippie. You act like you know *everything*." I took a deep breath and glared at him. He moved his head tightly through the blue darkness.

"You hardly know me. Don't start freaking out and cutting me up to fit in your little box," he said, and then he paused. "When I first met you I thought you were different. I guess you're just like the rest of them —you don't even look *around* you—"

"Well at least I'm not ugly."

What a stupid thing to say—something worthy of a spiteful child. With anyone else it would have been laughable, but with Conner, it was too real. The unspeakable truth had been spoken, and it heaved around us with the clouds of smoke. It hurt to hear him shuffle his legs along the ground, changing position. It hurt to sit there and feel the warmth of the flames next to my knee.

"Just because you think I'm ugly doesn't make it true," he said quietly. "Attractiveness is never true or false, anyway. It depends on who's looking. If you think you're going to make me self-conscious, you're wrong. This is what I look like."

I couldn't think of anything to say. My stomach pounded with both hunger and shame. I felt better when I was with Conner than I did with anyone else. It had been true from the beginning, but I didn't want to admit it. Why did I have to think so much about it? So what if he was—if I found him—ugly? I had this unreasonable craving for him to accept me, and I had just ruined my chances.

"Sorry. I'm sorry. I'm just tired. That was stupid, I didn't really mean it—"

"No, you meant it. But that's okay." His hand flew over the smoke as he swatted a mosquito away. His tone lightened. "We can still be friends."

We said goodnight. I crawled into my hut and laid upon the crunchy leaves. A family of long-legged spiders marched over my hand, but I managed to fall asleep anyway. I imagined myself at home, in my own bed, which in my memories was made of water.

When I woke up, Conner was on his back next to the dead fire. His eyes were squinted tight, and his forehead was wrinkled. He looked especially pale with the overcast morning hanging over him. The fire had shriveled into coals, but I could smell its ghost.

I walked away from him and looked up into the trees. They moaned in the wind, as though they were just waking up themselves. A crow bellowed from the branch of a hemlock tree. Its shiny beak made circles in the air. None of the smaller birds were singing; it was just the crow yelling out into the flat, quiet forest.

By the time I came back to the fire, Conner had picked more miner's lettuce and some red huckleberries. He steadily devoured them, staring off into the distance. I chose a translucent, orange berry from the pile, which rested on the dirt, and I wiped it on my pant leg. It tasted both sour and sweet. I ate a few more.

Neither of us said anything. I couldn't believe I had called him ugly out loud, to his face. I couldn't believe we were there.

"Did you ever want to be immortal?" I asked him suddenly. There was no need for small talk anymore; no need to ease into what we really meant. We had passed that point the moment we entered the wilderness together. Maybe even before.

"Who says we're not?" He looked up as he said it, tilting his head in a circle as the crow had done.

A melody surfaced, so powerful I couldn't hold it in, so powerful that I hummed it right then and there. It swept over me like exhaustion, both weighted and floating. I was beneath the trees and I was with Conner. There didn't seem to be much of a difference between the two.

"God, did you come up with that?" he asked after I had finished. "You should write it down. Do you keep a notebook with you?"

"No, I just remember everything."

"I guess if it's just a melody . . ."

"No, I have the harmony too. It's a piano concerto. At least, that's what it is in my head. It's in A minor."

"I wish I could hear inside your head," Conner said. "I've never been much of a composer." He looked at the ground, rubbing his knees absently.

"I guess anyone could say they have music in their head. How's anyone going to know if you're lying or not?"

"Are you saying you're lying, then?"

"No," I said. Then I smiled with my lips closed. "I'm saying I could be. You know at least the melody's real."

We finished off the berries and greens. The sun ate quickly through the clouds, and I started to sweat. We silently agreed to pack up and stood in tired unison.

"Should we take down the hut?" I asked him.

"No, just leave it. It's still part of the landscape, it'll return to the earth." Conner stroked the leaves and branches that had so easily sheltered me, and we left them behind.

# Chapter Eleven

The bobcat wouldn't leave my head; it wouldn't move or blink. It stared at me. Its eyes faded from yellow to gray to blue. I wanted so badly to look away, but I couldn't. To have a wild animal stare at me was . . . well, it wasn't supposed to happen. They were supposed to run away in fear, or at least attack. Even in dreams.

Then the bobcat raced in sultry circles. It uttered strange yelping noises. The dense fur around its neck fluffed up higher as it started to rain. *What are you doing out so early*, I heard. I wanted it to go away, and I felt like I needed to run.

I rose from my bed and drank a glass of ice water. I ate a bowl of cereal. I took a shower.

When I had come back into cell phone range earlier that day, several text messages from Skye had popped up. Where was I, she wanted to know, and what was I doing that weekend? I replied that I had been on a hike. And that was all I said.

I sat on the edge of my bed. Suddenly I regretted my decision not to buy a T.V. for my apartment. But why did I want to fill my head with dull advertisements? Catchy commercial jingles were the last thing I needed to spend money on.

The lighting in my apartment felt overcast. It was always dark, even on the brightest and sunniest of days. I finally fell asleep with the desk lamp on. Resting my head against a pillow instead of my hand was a warm joy. My shoulders were blissfully free from gnats and mosquitoes.

What came to me in the night were visions of the trees I'd walked past on the hike. Ponderosa pine, with their cracked bark and dry needles. Western hemlock, dressed in billowy green. They were a mix of the east and the west sides of the mountains; mostly east with a little western foliage still pushing toward the sunrise.

In my dream I walked past the trees again, reliving the day, only this time I held a large, cardboard box in my arms. For some reason I couldn't set it down, even though my muscles felt ready to snap.

Dead leaves crunched louder with each step. When I came to a pond, I saw the trees reach out for the sun. The moon spiraled into the zenith until it absorbed half the sky. I stopped to watch. Only then, when the wind was still over the dark water, was I allowed to throw down the box. The cardboard ripped against the rough shore of the pond. Moonlight bounced off of its exposed, shining surface. I crouched next to it and tore off the rest of the packaging. Inside was a brand new television.

All the shadows fled my eyes. I woke up to find my sheets in a bundle on the floor. The studio felt quiet, small, and dense. It was always The Studio in my head, back then. That way it was more than just a one room apartment.

I called Skye and we met for lunch at the cafeteria. She wore chunky hipster glasses with no glass in the frames. I wore jeans and a purple sweatshirt. We bought sandwiches and sat at a table near the window, although there were many more tables free because it was Sunday. Most students ate off-campus on the weekends, especially the upperclassmen.

"Okay. So there's this guy," Skye began. "He's in my biology class and he is *so* hot. Oh my *god*. Like, I've never seen anyone so hot up close. And we've talked a few times, and he's not, like, a total douche bag or anything. So I was starting to think I liked him."

"Oh my gosh! When did this happen?" I shrieked. "Have you been out on a date yet?"

"No, no. Well, maybe. I don't know if it was really a date. We just went out for coffee like a week ago, and then we had dinner last night. But—god, don't look so excited—I'm really not sure how much I'm into him. I guess I don't really *need* to know yet, but I thought, since he's so hot—I thought I would know right away."

"What don't you like about him?"

"That's the thing. I don't even know. I just don't know if there's that spark. How do you even know if you like a guy?" Skye creased her eyebrows together. "I haven't even had a boyfriend yet. Not a real one. I mean, I've kissed guys, and we've made out and stuff, but that doesn't count. It hasn't been a real relationship."

I nodded, chewing the dry bread of my sandwich. "Have you kissed him yet?"

"Not yet. I thought he'd pretty much be all over me when we got back from dinner, but I guess he's more of a gentleman than that. It's refreshing, you know? He even paid for me."

She stared at her hands, which were spread out on the table like delicate fans, each finger splayed wide.

"I guess you know you like someone when you think about him all the time, when you can't get him out of your head," I offered, my voice sounding stiff. I wasn't supposed to know about that sort of thing. She didn't expect me to. I didn't expect myself to. And yet, I felt like I knew something. It was as though I was pretending to know less than I did. "And I guess you should really look forward to hanging out with him . . . that sort of thing."

Skye swallowed a mouthful of her sandwich, and she took a sip of water. Ice cubes chimed against the glass as she set it back on the table. Her shoulders dropped, matching the creased expression on her face.

"I don't know. I definitely like hanging out with him. And who knows if he even likes me. He still has to ask me out again."

"Yeah. That's the hardest part is knowing whether they like you. Guys have it easy. They get to choose whoever they like, and take action, but all we can do is sit around and wait for someone to come after us," I said, my voice dying down as Skye stared at me.

"Do you . . . like anyone?"

"Not really."

"Not really?"

I didn't even know what I was saying. My head felt tight and I wanted to leave, despite Skye's kind eyes smiling from behind her black frames. The metal clang of pots and pans crashed from the nearby kitchen. The air conditioner beat down heavily on us. I glanced out the window. A rhododendron bush sat right outside of it. Beyond that was a parking lot, shining black in the crude autumn sun.

"Who is he?" Skye leaned forward.

"There's no one."

"Come on, *tell* me. I can see it in your eyes! That's good if you like someone. It's good for you, you know? It makes you bigger. Don't worry, I won't tell anyone."

Just then Sandal Girl walked up to our table. She balanced a veggie burger on her lunch tray, carrying a striped, woven bag in her other hand.

"Arianna!" Skye chirped. "Come sit with us."

Sandal Girl gently arranged her things on the table. She smoothed back her yellow sundress before sitting down.

"What's up, guys?" she asked with her mouth full of the beige, meatless patty.

"Are you a vegetarian?" I asked.

"Sometimes," she nodded.

They talked for awhile about their own things, stealing occasional glimpses at me as if to make sure I was still there.

"I'm in the mood to blaze," Skye told Sandal Girl. She rested her forehead on her hand. "But I've got all of this shit to do for school."

"Oh, Skye, do you guys play in front of the panel on the same day for violin as for piano?" I asked. "'Cause it's coming up soon, are you ready?"

"Oh, I don't know. I'm playing some Mendelssohn piece. Should be pretty easy."

Sandal Girl typed eagerly into her phone. She sucked in her lips until the lines around her mouth stood out.

"Okay, yeah, Arianna, I know we're lame," Skye shouted with a laugh. "Are you guys ready to go?"

We left the cafeteria and joined the sky. Evening was coming and it made me feel empty. I thought of the night before, when we had been completely alone with the air and the fire and the bobcat. I thought of how much the daylight had meant to me once it had so eagerly vanished.

Skye and Sandal Girl were off to smoke marijuana in the park again. The trees, to them, were a curtain. As she turned to leave, Skye whispered to me, "Go for it."

I knew she was talking about the guy I supposedly liked. And I was beginning to think that maybe . . . maybe she was right.

# Chapter Twelve

Conner hadn't texted me since our night in the forest. I waited three days afterward, checking my phone every half hour to make sure I hadn't missed it. I finally realized he may be waiting for me to text *him*.

I shook my head as I remembered the moment I had called him ugly. Was he mad? When he had dropped me off at my apartment, I had mumbled "goodbye" and "thanks" through my exhaustion. It has been a quiet hike out of the forest, and an even quieter car ride.

My imagination sometimes contorted Conner into a faceless voice, sometimes into an even-featured mountain man. Either way, his face was much handsomer in my memories, and it was easy to think I might like him. I texted him a simple greeting.

As I waited for a reply, I gathered my laundry into the hamper. The building's communal laundry room was empty. I shoved my dirty clothes into a machine and sat on the scratchy waiting chair. It was a concrete room on the ground floor, no windows. I blasted Liszt from my phone speakers and tapped my foot. Against the ticking of the laundry machine, it sounded hollow and frail.

How would Conner interpret such a difficult piece? I was sure it would be far from perfection, but magic nonetheless.

Just then my phone buzzed, interrupting the waltz. It was him:

*Hi. How are you?*

*I'm good, I replied. I had fun on our hike.*

*You did? Because you seemed furious.*

*Haha No, I was just scared at first. But it was a lot of fun. We should go again sometime.*

*Yeah. I'm busy with midterms and stuff though. Later on in the term.*

*Sounds good.*

Why didn't he sound enthusiastic? Was he really mad at me still? I turned the track to Mozart's symphony number forty in g minor. My stomach clenched at the thought of my piano recital. It was only a week away. We weren't graded on the difficulty of our piece, or the length, but on our precision and our musicality—at least in our first year.

We were expected to progress throughout our education, achieving near-concert level upon graduation.

Caroline wanted me to "play it safe" with one of Bach's inventions.

"A flawless performance of something *easy* is more impressive than forcing your way through something . . . too advanced," she said, glancing at my fingers. "Let's not delve into Rachmaninoff yet." She laughed.

But I could play Rachmaninoff. I could play Chopin's Ballades, and Beethoven's hardest sonatas. I could listen to anything and play it by ear. I could compose my own creations with my eyes closed, or conduct a symphony in my mind. I had been called a prodigy by all my childhood piano teachers.

How could she not see it?

"I've played Rachmaninoff," I stated, my voice flat.

"Well we're at a higher level now, aren't we? It's not about just playing the notes anymore. The phrasing, the tone, the accents—it needs to be the whole package." She looped her springy blonde hair behind her ears.

Bach it was. I hardly even needed to practice before I had it perfect. The melody was clear, jumping from right to left as each hand quarreled. As I played, I listened to it, and I floated with it. It was all I could do.

I saw Conner in class later that week. He was sitting near the front with a spot open next to him.

"Hey," I whispered. The professor had already quieted the class.

"Hello." Conner stared at the front of the classroom. His ankle rested on his knee.

For some reason I'd expected him to match my dreams; to have shed his ugly skin, resized his nose, and sculpted his jaw line. He kept his hands folded on his knee. Certainly they were his best feature. His nails were dirty but his skin looked unblemished and strong. Like a true pianist his fingers refused to stretch straight, always bent at the knuckle.

"How are your midterms going?" I asked him as we walked away after class. "Are you busy? Want to go get some lunch?"

"I'm just going to say it now. I don't like you that way." Conner licked his lips and looked away.

"What—what way? Are you still mad at me for what I said? Because—"

"No. I just thought you should know now. To make it easier on both of us. Let's just be friends."

I blinked repeatedly to find something to stare at. Anything but Conner's fixed gaze.

"Okay . . ." my voice was unavoidably heavy. I wanted

to laugh and tease him for his presumptuousness, but I couldn't fake it. Neither of us would be fooled, and it was already too late to save myself from embarrassment.

How did he know? How did he know so quickly and so easily when I had just remarked on his *ugliness* the other day? We hadn't even seen each other since then. Was it just the texting?

How could someone as nearly *deformed* as Conner not be infatuated with me? I wasn't unattractive. If I dressed up, I might even be slightly above average.

And why did I even think I liked him in the first place? He was hideous and weird and he had gotten me stranded in the woods.

"Don't worry," I said as I crossed my arms. "I have no problem with that."

# Chapter Thirteen

Why had I never had a boyfriend, I asked the bathroom mirror? My hair was smooth, shoulder-length, and rarely out of place. My skin was fairly even and looked healthy. There was a tiny mole on the edge of my jawbone that I thought added character.

My features were pretty at best, although not universally appreciated. It depended on who was looking. No one would ever call me beautiful.

My body was thin, well-proportioned, five foot five. I was no gorgeous model, no standout, undeniably lovely hottie, but I was average. Pleasantly average.

How could Conner not like me. How. How. How. What was wrong with me that an ugly boy didn't even—I needed to stop thinking about it. Too bad the nocturne kept echoing in my head, just the way he had played it.

A week quickly passed without word from Conner. We had our math midterm, so it was easy to sit in the back of the classroom, away from him. I knew we were supposed to be friends, but I couldn't bear it. Not yet.

The more I thought of him, the more he seemed like an evil menace. It was his fault. I'd done nothing.

Part of me wanted to tell Skye the whole thing, just to have someone to tell, but she would probably only make it worse and cackle at me for liking someone so unattractive. I couldn't tell Jessie or Sarah from back home, either. I hadn't talked to them for months. And Hallie . . . of course I couldn't tell Hallie.

So I tried to concentrate on school instead; on music. I spent hours in the glass practice rooms, committing Bach to the deepest form of finger-memory. To stop thinking I forced myself to stop feeling. I had nothing against Bach's inventions, but they weren't the release I needed. What I really wanted was something heavy and passionate, not smart and orderly.

When the day came, I cut my fingernails so short they ached. I dressed in a black, knee-length pencil skirt and flowy cream blouse. I visualized the performance, each note, each pulse, blending to build a long line of musical thought.

The room was dark except for the stage and the judge's table. Other students sat within the velvet rows of the auditorium, huddled unseen in the feathery depths of the shadows.

Caroline, wearing a tight red dress too long for her, came up to me. She clutched a notebook to her chest and waved it around as she talked.

"Good, you're just in time. Do you have your sheet music?"

I held up the stack of paper.

"Good. Go give it to the judges over there," she said hurriedly. "Then go backstage because you're the third one on. I'll meet you back there."

There were three judges, two women and one man, all elderly. It was just a shaky fold-up table they sat at, covered in a black tablecloth. Both the women wore pearls and burgundy red lipstick, and one had a treble clef pin above her breast. All of them wore black. They nodded curtly and continued whispering to each other as I handed them the photocopied scores.

I met Caroline behind the curtains.

"Okay, so let's just remember that you've practiced this a million times," she said gently, hanging her neck down with her eyebrows extended. "You've done all you can do to learn it technically, and now it's time to connect with it artistically. Really feel the music. Listen to it. Remember to pay attention to dynamics."

She rubbed her hands together. Her fingernails were painted red. They were chipping in little squares at the very tip.

Onstage was a grand piano; a new Steinway with the sound let to drift out the top. Every cough and every sigh could be heard from up there. The first student introduced herself and her piece. She skipped a few notes, but otherwise did a nice job with the first movement of a Mozart sonata.

"So are you nervous at all?" Caroline asked me. She looked around at the other students and their teachers, waiting in a line to go on. Conner wasn't up yet. He was probably still in the audience.

"No," I said. "I've performed so many times, I don't even get nervous anymore."

"Mmm. Okay just—okay, the next guy's almost done. Get up there, get ready to go on!" She nudged my shoulder toward the curtain.

The last guy came back, sweat dripping down his goatee. I pushed through the dusty, heavy curtains, and into the yellow stage lights. Past the round, wooden edge of the stage was a dark wall. The air in front of me was empty. I couldn't even see the judges, though they sat close enough to rest their legs on the edge.

My black flats tapped a plastic rhythm as I walked in front of the piano. I announced myself to the flying flecks of dust, then I sat down. For a moment I stared at the keys with my hands in my lap. I breathed in a huff of overused air, felt the silky, varnished starting notes, and played. My memory led me easily through the piece.

I thought suddenly of Conner; of the Beethoven sonata he would passionately play. I thought of running lost through the forest, of leaping over streams, of staring into the expansive black pupils of hawks and bobcats.

Caroline underestimated me. I clenched my jaw as I came to the easy piece's conclusion.

I was better than this. I was better than Caroline or Conner. If I had only made it into a better school, wouldn't they see that? Wouldn't everyone then acknowledge my genius?

The bobcat stepped circles through my head. Its flat, fluffy paws clawed over everything else.

When I came to the last note, I didn't stop. I went into my own composition. It was as unlike Bach as possible. All the colors changed to gold and sparkling yellow, pouring over me like a waterfall had opened in the ceiling above the stage. I tilted my head up to it and drank in the sweet water.

The audience clapped slowly and lightly. I bowed and returned to Caroline's side. Her hands were over her eyes.

"May," she whined, shaking her head. "Oh, May. What was that? You had it perfect and then—what was that weird modern stuff you started playing? Whatever it was, they'll add it on as an error to the Bach piece because you didn't tell them you were playing it. What—what could you possibly have been thinking? Why would you do that? All the work we put into it. You won't pass. You know this affects your grade, right? I'll have to ask them if you can retake it, and even then you can only get a C."

Weird modern stuff.

"I don't know what I was thinking."

Weird modern stuff.

Caroline opened her mouth and sighed. She shook her head some more, staring at the ground.

"Okay, well, go see how you did."

The judges handed me their remarks without any expression on their weathered faces. Deviation from the score, into a random configuration of notes, at the expense of the performance, read one. Otherwise, great tone and fantastic phrasing. The rest had similar comments. Bach was great, they said. Why did I ruin it with whatever nonsense I added on?

That nonsense was my entire essence. It was my definition, my goal, my life's purpose. How dare they take it away from me? Tears washed my eyes as I realized what a great embarrassment I'd wrought upon myself. How dare they?

I had nothing left and it was dark and everyone must be looking at me. I left the auditorium without another word to Caroline.

My chest was tight. I imagined the judges going home and wiping off their lipstick on coarse napkins. They would laugh to their husbands about the crazy girl who had sabotaged her own performance.

Really it was they who had sabotaged it; them and all the others in the audience. They were the ones who curled their darkness into a weapon, and hurdled it under the stage lights. They were the ones to blame, and now their darkness rested within me, too.

# Chapter Fourteen

"It's alright, honey. You can retake it, right?"

"Yeah, but I get marked down . . . Why can't I come home? I could go to the community college instead. It would be way cheaper."

"Just wait out the term and then we'll talk about it. Okay?"

"I don't see how I can keep composing, or even playing music, after this. I just don't see how. That's all I ever wanted. And now . . . I don't even know . . . now I have nothing."

"I know I don't know much about music, but I love the songs you make up, May. They're so simple but they still have so much feeling behind them. I've never heard anything like it."

"They weren't impressed. They hated it."

"They were just surprised. It was the wrong time. Just don't give up. You can never give up. Remember Shelley Bernstein? Who took group classes with you for a few years when Matilda was teaching? Her mom came up to me at the store the other day and said Shelley still talks about your senior recital last year. She even started composing so she can do the same when she graduates."

I released air from my nose, half a laugh, half an exhale.

"Okay? Don't worry, everything will be fine. Now, love you honey, I have to go make dinner."

"Love you mom."

"'Night. And don't forget to call Hallie!"

"I won't."

"Alright. Bye, sweetie."

I threw my phone into the carpet and bit my shaking lip. My eyes closed and I wanted it to stay that way, buzzing in the soft lines of darkness. It wasn't just the absence of light but my eyelids themselves that I was seeing; they were illuminated red against the first spasms of sunset. The sky was trying to leak through the cracks in the blinds, so I drew them up and opened the window.

Breath. I concentrated on each breath rising into my shoulders. My whole body felt heavy and sharp. Each step was thorns and blisters. I wanted to burn something or rip off my skin, or perhaps scream into a canyon during a thunderstorm. I wanted to shoot darts into the hands of the judges, and to chop off Caroline's hair with rusty, squeaking scissors as she slept. And Conner . . . I couldn't even think of anything.

By the time I could unclench my molars and lower my shoulders, the sun had gone away. I knelt on the floor and picked up my phone. Standing next to the window, I dialed Hallie's number.

"Hello?" Her voice was high, stretching without enthusiasm.

"Hi Hallie. Happy birthday."

"Thanks. So . . . how's school going?"

"Did Mom tell you already?"

"Yeah. I just hung up with her and Dad."

"So you already know how school's going, then. And on top of that, there's this guy—" I paused. I listened to Hallie breathing on the other end. "We were hanging out and stuff, and he realized I liked him before I even said anything. And he said he doesn't like me back."

"Oh, May, that happens all—"

"No, it's not just that. He's . . . well, he's not very cute. I know that sounds really mean, but that's actually the nicest way I can put it."

Hallie was quiet.

"So even an ugly guy doesn't like me," I said. "I'm undateable, and I'm never going to make it as a composer, and I hardly have any friends, and they're always smoking pot and drinking and . . ."

Hallie was still quiet.

"It'll all work out," she finally said. "Remember that one time you picked up my violin when I first started playing—oh and I'd been struggling with it for months trying to figure out where the pitches were and how to use the bow—and you picked it up and you played it on your first try. Just like that. No figuring it out, no sight reading. You just picked it up and played ode to joy by ear on your first try. It's just one bad experience. Seriously, May. Get over it."

"I have stuff to do. Happy birthday. Bye."

"Night. Don't do drugs."

I sat on the floor with my legs crossed. My eyes shut and I rested my fingers on my lips. The carpet felt like a sponge. Each loop of fabric was clearly visible and worn to a wiry thinness. The refrigerator clicked and sputtered. A plane shook the windows as it flew overhead.

The moon graced my legs with its pastel fire. It filled the frame of the window, palling the black sky around it to a weary purple. From a vague distance I could see the hills, deep blue without the sun on them, mounds of color without any facets exposed. I imagined the branches of pines waving calmly in the moonlight. I imagined the birds nestled close to their trunks, seeking warmth in the trees.

How many times had I rested my head against the trunks of my own cedar trees? How many times had I looked up into them? The red bark coated my hair as I watched the branches. They didn't quiver; they were too heavy and regal for that. When the sweet air touched them they sang along in harmony. Thick and scaly, the leaves sang of wind and water. They sang of secrets known only to those closest to the sun. I listened on days when the wind could be seen but not felt.

Some nights I looked through my window to count their great, humped shadows, and to watch the moon wash them brown. I loved the cedars, I decided, more than any other conifer. But that was only because I knew them so well.

There was always something to be seen in the sky, wasn't there? A crow, a cloud, a cottonwood's glimmering crown at the beginning of spring. Or the moon . . .

My phone buzzed. Skye. She had been in the audience. She'd seen it all. Violinists were scheduled for later in the afternoon, and she'd come early to watch me.

Did you still get a good score? she asked.

I have to retake it, I replied.

Bummer. I know what will take your mind off it. You

better come or I'll drag you out I swear.

Haha ok, I'll be there, I responded. Because, really, what was my alternative? I needed to find someone better than Conner. I needed a new brain.

My back remained curved and sullen for the rest of the night. I painted my fingernails neon green. The smell dampened the air of The Studio with oily poison. Each stroke was careful and precise. The brush cut smooth lines into the color. There was no need to worry about it chipping off on the keys. Not for the next few days.

The party was at Sandal Girl's house. She lived with two other girls in a duplex with a hole in the roof. I wasn't sure which girls were her roommates—the house was full of feather hair-extensions and studded nose piercings.

A plastic table held tortilla chips, puffy cheetos, salsa, and chocolate chip cookies. Next to it was a great blue cooler overflowing with beer cans. Their windows were clothed in what appeared to be old, yellow quilts. Plastic bins, filled with text books, tennis shoes, and headbands, were pushed to the wall to make room for beer-handed mingling.

I hadn't gone out since the previous disaster. The music was the same—repetitive bass took hold of the ceiling.

Although it was only a thin sliver, I could see out the hole in the roof. The sky was there, as always, and the sun had just left it. It was a cold night. The frosts of November were approaching.

"I feel like you're always judging me," a girl behind me said. She paused to crunch a tortilla chip. "Every time I say something I can just feel it."

"Well I am judging you. I judge everyone. You are so funny. I've never met anyone like you," her friend responded. "Who doesn't even know what REI is? And you've never heard of Macklemore? Who are you? You're like an alien."

They ate some more cheetos. Their jaws worked away at the foamy chips. I moved forward and grabbed a handful of tortilla chips. The alien looked down at her sparkly Vans, then at her companion's Tom's brand shoes.

"You know what? You're a bitch," she said soothingly. Quietly.

She faced me and I backed away from the snack table. Where was Skye? I pushed through the growing crowd, into the kitchen. Skye and Sandal Girl each held two six-packs of beer. Their arms struggled against the weight.

"May, go put these in the cooler," Sandal Girl said. She thrust a box toward my chest.

"It's not my party."

"Jeez, I'll take care of it. Why did you even come if you're in such a shitty mood?" Sandal Girl lunged into the living room.

Why did I? None of the guys were coming up to me. I forced myself to stand near Skye's circle, but I really wanted to crouch in the corner and watch the others. Watch them sway and call it dancing. Watch them laugh about the last time they were high. Watch them melt away to the bedrooms to get high again. It smelled like marijuana. Dirt and sweat. The guys wore bright tank tops, the girls wore tights skirts and cleavage. The guys left their hands on the girls' shoulders, moving them, whispering at their noses until the girls swore.

The song changed. It pumped and rang. A girl screamed. Three guys responded. Their screeches were guttural howls, primal in a way meant only to be outrageous.

I told Skye I was going, and I left. This time I could ride the bus back by myself; Sandal Girl's house was right on the bus line. It was empty, except for an old man in the back. His stomach covered his legs. I sat forward on the bus seat so my thighs wouldn't stick to the plastic. My hair still smelled like the party. I brushed it behind my shoulders and opened the window a crack. The night fell in, sweet and clean.

As the old man limped to the front of the bus, he bitterly grasped the poles lining the aisle. His sandals were too big for his socked feet, and they slapped against the rubbery grooves in the floor. He glared at me as he passed. His wind smelled of cigarette smoke and vinegar.

My stop came quickly. The engine and the air from the window cloaked my ears, filling me with enough noise to dissuade my thoughts. There was light on us. It made the outside even darker than before.

I walked past the old man. As I heaved myself down the first stair, toward the sidewalk alight with bird poop and a crushed water bottle, I considered turning around.

What if I stayed on the bus? What if I rode it to its farthest reaches? After that I could hitchhike, I could walk. I could hop onto a moving train, then spend the night camping in the wilderness. I could see everything. All the sky would be my home. I would sing to myself as I walked the canyonlands and forests. In my music I would capture the rocky hills smoking red at sunset, the fields of beargrass blowing white in the mirrors of hidden mountain lakes, the great geese migrating on the plains in glossy, gray clouds. It was right there. Everything was right there.

But my feet had already fled. The bus driver said nothing. He drove away. I stood on the sidewalk. My eyes adjusted to the unblemished night. It felt dull in the back of my eyes. Everything felt dull.

# Chapter Fifteen

I retested the next week, and I did fine. New set of judges. Same piece. C+. Good work, good work. Nice sense of timing, perfect sculpting of the melody, amazing technique. It's a shame we can't give you an A.

I left the theater and stared at the floor as I walked.

"I liked your last performance better." Conner was leaning against the wall in the empty hallway.

I cleared my throat, half laughing, half snorting, half sucking in my cheeks because they still ached from being stretched into a stage-smile. One of the judges walked past holding a cardboard coffee cup. He smiled at us. After he turned the corner I stepped closer to Conner.

"You did?"

"It was just like what you hummed when we were in the forest." Conner grinned and his whole face puffed up with ruddiness. "It was just like it. Like the trees. It was alive."

Once again I laughed.

"Seriously," he looked at me closely. His eyebrows frilled around the edges, curving upward in wiry tufts. His eyes were especially blue, even in the shadowed hallway light, and they stood out against his white t-shirt. "I feel like I know you now."

He leaned forward, and those fat, lopsided lips . . . I was falling through the floor. I was tangled in a mat of vines; in his dry, brown hair. My eyes closed. Our arms didn't touch as we kissed. It didn't seem to matter.

"That is how you speak," he whispered. "That is who you are."

I wasn't sure if he was talking about my music or the kiss. Another pianist walked past us. I pretended to look through my bag. Conner refused to move his gaze from my face.

"God, Conner. You're so weird. I don't even know what you're talking about half the time," I giggled, licking my lips. Then I shook my head. "I thought—okay, didn't you just want to be friends?"

Conner took my hand in his. He pulled me down the hallway. We escaped into the overcast morning. A song sparrow's chant, like a stream, poured from the naked tree next to the music building.

Our hands were neither hot nor cold. They were wrapped together like wet leaves fallen upon the dirt, the way they cling and cannot be separated, or else transparentness will overcome them. And so we walked down the road, along the ditch where no cars could see us. We crunched the hay-like nests of wild carrot and the frail backbones of common vetch.

We came to the park, where we sat at the base of an oak tree, rolling our bottoms over dusty acorns. There were brown leaves left on the spidery branches. Not many. In the distance was a group of Steller's jays. They sang for us in gritty, nasal hiccups.

I looked over at Conner, who was just sitting there, breathing. He inhaled the damp crust of the earth and the clouds above us. He inhaled the wind coming from the river, far in the distance. His face was a crushed bundle of aluminum. He stared away with flushed intensity. I wanted to know why he had progressed so suddenly from pure rejection to adoration. To a kiss. A kiss. But I didn't want to wake him from the dream.

"Why did you kiss me?" I finally, bitterly, asked, after I felt the hours pass. My voice was soggy. I ran my fingers over the chipping green polish coating them.

"Because I wanted to kiss you," he said.

And I believed him. I believed it really could be as simple as that.

# Chapter Sixteen

We watched the sun set every evening that week. I wore my thick, down coat, red wool mittens, and a knit hat, and I was still trying not to shiver. Conner wore a thin, green hoodie. He wrapped my hand again between his unclothed palms. We sat on the bench next to the library, facing the mountains. There was a light dust of icy snow on the grass, but not enough to cover it up.

The sun drew color out of the line of peaks, like dandelions closing their heads at night. It seemed the sun left us earlier than it should, even for November. The mountains stole him. They always seemed calm and nurturing, the line of soft, white giants.

"I'll never get tired of it," I sighed. "It's so pretty."

Conner nodded.

My Ugg boots crunched into the frost as I stood. "But I *am* getting cold," I said.

"This is nothing. It's going to rain tomorrow," Conner said.

"How do you know?"

"The wind is changing."

I laughed. "You're right, and the sunset wasn't even very red."

"What?"

"Red sky at night, sailor's delight. Red sky in the morning, sailor's warning. Haven't you ever heard that?"

He shook his head and laughed. "It's pink. Pink always means sun the next day."

When we made it back to my apartment he kissed me again, just as quickly as before. We left each other. I closed the door quietly, leaning in until I felt it click into the frame.

Home again. Alone again. I stepped heavily toward my bed, leaned down, and selected a folder from the pile on the floor. It was fat, ripping at the divider because of so much stress.

I coughed, and then sighed. My breath was just warming up. I selected one sheet of paper from the folder. In my hands it felt tired and powerless. Just a flimsy, spoiled piece of paper, written up with staccato sixteenth notes and abrupt eighth-note rests. It was what I had once called music. Only weeks before it had been the beginnings of something marvelous, something to share.

Now it was worn shit in my hands, ready to be torn coolly into long strips. I felt each fiber pull away from the next. I heard the piece burn slowly in my head and saw great rivers wash away the lines of the staff.

I was the best in my hometown; the best composer and pianist that had ever lived there. My teachers told me so, my fellow students admitted it, my parents insisted it was true. But I finally realized, sulking there with wrinkled paper in my hands, that that was only because my town had a population of 3,200. It was a mix of vineyards and sheep grazers and grass seed farms, with some suburb-y neighborhoods on the side. There was no great history of music there, and there were few enough people to make the chance of talent unlikely. Of course I seemed better than I really was.

Maybe I could learn to be a better composer. Maybe the judges and my teacher were just subjectively unappreciative—after all, Conner liked my music. I breathed in deeply, but it didn't ease my stomach.

Soon the floor was littered with evil white strips, like dirty flakes of snow. I didn't know what to do so I went to the kitchen and grabbed potato chips. Half the bag was gone within minutes. I rolled the salt around my tongue, and I cursed the crunch as it reminded me of drums.

Finals were soon over, tiring and uneventful. My parents drove out to pick me up for our month-long break. They already looked older than they had at the end of the summer. Both of them wore sweatshirts and jeans. My mom's hair looked limp, and my dad's forehead seemed ready to crack into wrinkles. They were almost a photograph; not quite real, not quite whole.

We hugged. I placed my duffel bag in the trunk.

"Oh, can we give someone a ride?" I asked them as we opened the car doors.

"Oh, sure. Where do they live?" they responded in overlapping, high-pitched tones.

"Forty-five minutes from our house, towards the coast, is that okay? Otherwise he has to wait here for three days until his friend can come and pick him up. He has a car but it died the other day and he hasn't had a chance to get it fixed."

"I guess," my mom said. "But we can't do this every time. You know how far we have to drive. *Both ways.* That's six hours."

I texted Conner. He came around the corner with a backpack on one shoulder. I made the introductions. My parents shook hands with him, one at a time. He was taller than my mom, but they still looked down on him with wide eyes as though he was a little boy.

The car started. It was warm away from the wind and frosty earth.

"So your little apartment was okay with just you in there? You weren't scared or anything, May?" my dad asked from the driver's seat.

"No, it was fine."

"Did you get any grades back yet?" asked my mom without turning around.

"No, not yet. Did you?" I asked Conner.

"Some of them."

I breathed in the car smell, a mix of my house, of laundry, and of soda.

"When are you getting your car fixed?" I asked. "Did you take it to the place yet?"

"Actually, I don't think I'm going to get it fixed."

"Why?"

"It's . . . not necessary. None of us really need to do all this driving. We could walk or bike or take the train. It would reduce emissions and stop supporting the auto-industrial complex. The only thing is getting to places too far to bike to, where there's no public transit. That's why we need to design our cities so everything's more compact. So far they've catered to the car, and it's so heavily subsidized . . ."

"What's your major again?" asked my dad.

"Music. Piano performance," Conner said.

"Not environmental science?" my dad laughed.

"I don't want to reduce *everything* into something small, something on a page that I have to memorize. I can live it without them ripping it apart."

My dad was silent. He nodded his head and glanced back at us through the rear-view mirror.

"Well, sorry for supporting the auto-industrial complex. Like you said, some of us have no other option." My dad laughed again, and then he turned on the radio. It was a commercial advertising a free steak with your next oil change.

"I think," said Conner, "that when I go home at the end of spring term I'm going to walk. You know, backpack it. I'm going to walk the whole way."

"Good luck," my dad coughed. "That'll take you two *months.*"

"What are you going to do with all your stuff? Are you renting storage?" I asked.

"No, no. I'm subleasing my room in the duplex for the summer."

"Won't your roommate mind?"

"No, he doesn't care."

"But what about your stuff? Are you just going to leave it there?"

"Yeah. They can use it."

"All of it? Even your sheets, your towels?"

"Yeah. I won't need them over the summer anyway. There's more at home."

"Your clothes?"

"Okay," Conner turned his face from the window and looked at me. "I'll take some with me on the road and leave the rest. If it fits whoever rents from me, they can borrow it."

"Wow," I said. There seemed nothing more to say so I looked at the radio, listening both to the 80's music playing and to what whirled within my head.

My mom was asleep. I could hear her breathing, deep and throaty. We remained silent as the hills became mountains around us, as the grassy white dust-fields sprouted pines, then hemlocks dwarfed by great bundles of snow. The world was muted by the constant gray sky above. I waited for the snow to melt away. It had lost its novelty with the dry frosts of the east. I wanted green again. Soon I had it.

We made our descent into the valley. It was raining. Always raining. The roads ran thick with cars. Maple and ash trees lining the freeways were rubbed invisible by the wind.

By the time we got to Conner's house, the sun was almost gone. We passed a gas station, a convenience store, a fire station, a school, and a row of little shops, all spread out from one another so long grass blew between them. The hills behind the town were half mined of their trees; the exposed dirt looked harsh and sore.

"Where's your house, Conner?" my dad asked as he paused at the barren stoplight.

"You know what, it's kind of hard to find. It's up a long driveway over there near the hills. I'll just get out here." He placed his backpack in his lap.

"Are you sure?" my mom turned around, her hair illuminated around her face by the setting sun.

"Yeah, it's fine." He tried the handle of the door, but it was locked. It clicked as my dad unlocked it. "Thanks for the ride."

"See you in a month." I smiled.

I watched him march behind the old buildings, with their paint peeling and their porches drooping. I could almost hear the soggy grass as he stepped on it. The rain had stopped but there would still be drops on every leaf. His knees would be soaked. The wind ran cold but he wouldn't care.

It's not like my parents knew we were dating. He couldn't have kissed me. But he left me with only a quick flash of his red-rimmed eyes. And then there was the car door and that was it. And that wasn't enough.

# Chapter Seventeen

It was too cold to sit outside for very long, so I stayed in. I texted Conner—good morning, how are you, did you get home okay—but he never replied. I figured he didn't have service in his town.

My piano didn't have enough spring to the keys and my fingers needed to work harder than they had at school. I crossed my legs at the bench, and I cracked my knuckles until they echoed off the wood. I spent two afternoons that way. For some reason I couldn't go outside and face the trees. I couldn't sing to them.

Then Hallie came home. Her friend dropped her off while our parents were at the supermarket. I opened the door for her and stood in the hallway while she shoved off her leather boots. She hugged me quickly, rubbing her bony shoulders into mine.

127

"Well, May," she said, squinting down at me. "How were finals?"

"They were fine. How were yours?"

"Yeah, they were fine, too, I guess. As fine as finals can be." She put her backpack, tote, and duffle bag back on, and heaved them into the living room. "Hey, how's that guy? The ugly guy?"

"Good. I kissed him." I laughed in a hiccupy sort of way and glanced behind me.

Hallie stood. She pulled her hair out of its bun, staring down at the matte wood floors with her eyebrows taut.

"I thought he didn't like you," she grunted.

"So did I. But he does now. We're . . . kind of dating."

"What did mom and dad say?"

"They don't know. We gave him a ride home, actually. But they don't know. Dad kept saying he was too intense."

The front door shook. My parents walked in with paper grocery bags at their sides. The sky was a deep, silvery pink, despite it being only four o'clock.

Once the food was put away I sat with them in front of the television. All four of us, our hips touching on the blue couch, our feet up on the coffee table. I itched the line where my hair met my neck. I tucked my phone between my legs and squinted at its screen during commercials.

Short days stained the skin beneath my eyes. The clouds

were balled up, worn, dry. I walked along the crusty windows and watched my lips as I smiled into the worn glass. My reflection followed me. I followed the wind; it told the trees to move their shadows against the white hallway.

But I refused to play. I couldn't. Every time I sat down at the piano my eyelid twitched or my ears popped or some other part of my body pulled me away. Or I would hear the kitchen sink colliding with metal, the empty crack of the house's corners, and I would wander away with my fists in the soft pockets of my hoodie.

There was music behind me.

Hallie's hair brushed the keys as she leaned over and played. She hadn't sat down at the piano for two years, maybe longer. At first she poked at middle C and the D next to it. She locked the joints of her first two fingers and dug them delicately into the wood. Then her wrists relaxed. Hallie still remembered how to lead with her arms flowing up the keyboard. Her fingernails clicked. They tapped against the worn, graying enamel of the keys as she played one of Bach's *Minuets*.

"I bet he plays piano too, doesn't he," she said. She rested her chin on her shoulder. The piece fell apart while her eyes rested on the floor. "You wouldn't date someone who wasn't as obsessed as you."

I shuffled down the hallway toward Hallie. Toward

the piano and the armchair next to it. Hallie's back looked too thin against the grand piano's curves. The bumps along her spine burst through her purple t-shirt. I wondered if I looked like that, too, when I sat there.

"Yeah. He's a piano major too." I sat at the very edge of the arm chair. The velvet seam rubbed through my cotton pant leg. "Mom kept saying he doesn't seem like a pianist."

"And he's ugly?"

"Yeah. I mean, no, not really ugly. He's just *different* looking. What's ugly? Who decides?"

Hallie nodded and muttered a small *mmm*. She pushed down the piano pedal without playing anything. It echoed emptily, metallically.

"Is he good?"

*"Good?"*

"Does he play piano *well?*"

I rubbed my eye and answered yes.

"Better than you?"

"Well, I've only heard him play once. Want to hear what he played?" I asked. I rose from the armchair and stood behind Hallie.

"Oh jeez, May. Okay."

We switched spots. I began with a B-flat, long and soft and ringing just right. The *Nocturne* came easily. It was like blue water overcoming me. It was the bobcat crouching low in the rain, breathing along with the heavy drops that hit the maple leaves. The fur of her paws was red from rusty streams bleeding over the earth, wild and running until roots consumed the clay.

"Oh, that one," Hallie exclaimed over the piano's fire. She edged back to the hall, filled with the blunt shadows of the overhead lights, and she walked away to the kitchen.

Matilda, my old piano teacher, was middle-aged, with brown hair forever in a low braid. She was short and wore seasonal pins on her shirt; Christmas trees, hearts, clovers.

"There are two ways to play," she told me. "Practice and performance."

While performing, you could never stop. Not if you stumbled, not if your hand cramped. You had to keep going when you were in that performance state of mind, even if no one was listening.

I stopped at the end of the next measure, and I followed Hallie into the kitchen. So much for a performance.

# Chapter Eighteen

I felt like I had reptile eyes. I felt like membranes closed over my pupils from the side and cloaked my vision in veins. Weeks.

They all just looked at me like they knew that I wasn't good enough. They all looked at me with this little laugh in their eyes, this little all-knowing smile that said "we know you don't belong here and you don't know what you're doing and you're not like us." It followed me beneath my shoes, stinking in my hair and burning my cheeks to a dull red-ivory. I couldn't look back at them without seeing it; the tilt to the eyes, the pity and the knowledge and the distance.

That distance could never be broken because I knew they had put it there. They knew I had put it there. We danced along the walls with our arms out but never grazing even each other's fingertips. We nodded at each other but avoided the eyes. Always avoid the eyes for too long, or else you'll see it.

Average. So much for average. My whole chest sank down and in. Thinking about school made me feel like I was less than average. Like I should be different.

I sat at home and watched the bright-colored commercials flicker without sound. My forest and my orchard and my fields were out there, and they were good. I just wasn't ready to go out to them. The thought of drizzle in my hair persuaded me to stay inside. One day I sent Conner a Christmas card, but, otherwise, I hardly did anything at all.

Christmas brought me music books and warm clothes. I didn't go outside because I didn't want my hands to dry and redden.

Weeks.

Then it was over.

Hallie left first, in a silver car full of friends. I could hear the rap music shaking before I saw the car come down our gravel driveway. Hallie waddled toward it with one backpack on her stomach and the other behind her. She was wearing a collared white shirt, dark jeans, and draping necklaces of beads. Her skin looked especially matte, especially thick and healthy. My dad carried her duffel bag out to the trunk. She hugged my parents lightly, afraid to grip them too hard.

"Good luck at school," she said to me. Her friends never turned down the music, not even to stick their heads out the window to say hello. Hallie whispered, with fruity gum in her mouth, "And good luck with ugly guy."

They left, driving north to the city.

The next day my parents drove me east. Up the hills, into the old-growth firs. Chains on the tires, snow and blown branches in the road. Down the hills, into the fire-burnt pines. The road sliced through everything and showed us walls on either side.

"Look at the mountain," I exclaimed as we came over the pass. It was the tallest of the peaks, stern and steady. It seemed almost patient, rising above the world in a thick wall of clouds.

"Pretty," my mom said.

"Yeah, that's nice," my dad said, hiccupping. "Nice."

The mountain deserved more than that, more than our words could give it. And yet it had everything it needed. Without our words or our eyes, the mountain would stand. Its roots would spread over the earth, the rocks, and the mossen rivers of the plateau. The sun would still set at its back. The winds would blow by with salt on their breath, and wash snow down gray-blue crevasses. Arrow-leaf balsamroot would still sprout yellow flowers on its foothills each spring.

When I looked at the mountain I saw the sky pulled down into a powerful triangle. It was benevolent, humming a deep and satisfied *mmm* as all great things did.

A headache developed between my eyes. It pressed against the inside of my forehead, over and over until my face felt bloodied. Long car rides made me sick when I was little. My mom used to let me lie down in the backseat of the car. I would watch the clouds that moved so fast out of the corner of the window. But my head always hurt for the rest of the day, for every moment until I fell asleep. I thought I had outgrown it.

The pain continued even after the car stopped, even after I felt the dry chill on my nose. It continued throughout the good-bye's, where I held my lips steady and drew water into my eyes; when I opened the door to my apartment and inhaled the fresh dust. I shoved my bag into the corner between my bed and the wall. My hands cupped over my elbows, crossed and goose-bumped. The heater wasn't on yet.

Once again I checked my phone. I left him ten text messages over break, all unanswered. Probably unopened. Hopefully *unopened*.

I decided to call him, just to see if he was there. It rang once after I clicked the green button. Then it rang again, a sound like a pleading spiral, and I hung up. The red button dropped down in pitch.

And then his name popped up on the screen. Incoming call.

"Hello?" I emptied the spit from my throat and dug my thumb into my forehead.

"Did you call me?"

"Yeah. Um. I just wanted to know if you were back at school."

"I'm still on the bus."

"What bus?"

"The greyhound bus," he said, and as he said it I heard voices behind him. They shouted and called like children.

"Oh, okay. Yeah. Well we should do something tomorrow. When you're back."

"Sure." The hiss of tires wrung out his tired voice.

"Hey, didn't you get my texts?"

"I didn't have--" he took a breath. "May. I just, I couldn't. There was too much to deal with. I'll tell you--I have to go."

"Oh . . . okay. Bye, Conner."

He echoed in my ear--his voice, his face, the way he must look against the tall, patterned bus seats. There was probably a stain by his thigh and a fat man sitting next to him. Conner's eyes would always be toward the window.

The next day my eyes were tight but my forehead was calm. I stood by the window and waited for Conner. My hair was curled into loose waves and my lips were cloaked in tinted lip balm. Conner walked up the stairs wearing a brown t-shirt. He looked different. Wider in the cheeks, and his hair was darker, or longer, or perhaps both.

"What is this?" I teased. "It's in the twenties."

He just smiled and skipped the last step, hopping up to me. He managed not to slip on the thick diamonds of ice.

"That's warm enough," he said.

We hugged, at first from the side, then facing each other. He was warm in the flushed way of fever. Up close I saw that the little hairs below his lip had grown fat.

I wasn't sure whether we should kiss, so I led him inside. He had never been in the studio, and I wondered for a moment whether I should have cleaned up a little. Dust and strange flecks of window-dirt clothed the plastic counters and the little table. My shoes were flung across my bedroom, remnants of closet re-organization. I thought with desperation of the bathroom. What would he think of my make-up cluttering the counter, of the hair tufts gathering in the corner of the tile floor?

The only place to sit was the kitchen. We sat with our elbows on the table. For awhile we talked about how fast the break had gone by, about our classes the next day. He kept looking away, at his hands or at the refrigerator as we spoke.

"It's all pointless." His pert, low mouth fell straight.

"What, school?"

"Everything. All of it. I don't know." He rocked his head forward twice. His eyes widened. "May, my grandfather died. Over the break."

"Oh my god—"

"No, it wasn't over the break. Before the break. Right after Thanksgiving, probably. We don't know because they just found him there. They just found him sitting there in his . . ." Conner bit his lip. He nodded again. "They found him in his house. It was an old house by the river. We always used to stay there overnight when we wanted to fish the next day. An old cabin-looking house right by the river. You could see the water out the window. You could even hear the fish jump if you left the window open.

"My grandma had cancer a few years ago and he's been there alone. No one even went up to check on him. Not for two weeks. That's how long he was sitting there before they found him. That's how long it took for them to notice. That's how little he meant."

I couldn't say anything. I ground my teeth into my lip, scraping away the lip balm.

"You're from a small town," he went on. "You know how it is, how everyone knows each other but it's still so easy to get lost."

"Oh my god, Conner. I'm sorry."

"And," he chuckled deeply, then inhaled sharply, "how everyone says, 'ah, he's fine', until they want something. Shit. *Shit.* God. You could hear the fish splash when they jumped out of the current. And we had this rope up on the cottonwood tree so we could swing into the water."

Both of us stared at the same point in the table, right in the middle where I had spilled a little mustard before break. It was crusty now, dark green at the edges. I worried suddenly that my apartment smelled--what did it smell like? Old air and vanilla body mist?

Conner scooted forward on his seat. He rubbed his hands against his thighs.

"I saw him like that. I *saw* him like that. I don't know. I should probably go." He walked to the door and stood under it, hunched. When he blinked his stubby eyelashes glued together. The sides of his nostrils were red in the opaque light of the window.

I thought I should rub his arm, or rest my chin on his chest.

His fingers were already extended toward the doorknob. He swallowed loudly.

"See you tomorrow?" I asked with my hands in the pockets of my sweater.

He nodded. His cheeks trembled. I waited at the

doorway until he moved beyond my vision. The wind came in and sucked around my torso, between my legs.

All I wanted was for the music to fall over me like that. I wanted it to sculpt around me and cover up my face. I wanted it to continue after it had left me, and float away into the juniper trees. A car brushed by. I closed the door to shut out the dirty noise.

# Chapter Nineteen

Skye drove us to the mall in the next town over. Her parents bought her a car for Christmas. It was completely electric, and a bright, sparkly blue. Wearing sunglasses, she wove expertly over the thin coating of snow on the road.

"Finally, my own car," she groaned with her chin in the air. "Finally, some goddamn freedom."

She parked and slammed the door shut.

We entered the thick heat that smelled like medicine and cleaning chemicals. The floor was white tile with orange puddles every few steps. My sneakers felt weightless against it. Skye inched off her sunglasses and dropped them in her brown hobo bag.

Two women with lumpy backs walked past us, their thick legs wrapped in sweatpants. A girl crouched behind a trash can while her mom yelled for her. Her voice matched the clear space between the clouds outside, those little dips of blue that looked like deep, clear water. The girl squinted her wide-spaced eyes and leaped out to pull her mother's long, dark hair.

Skye chose a store with blue mannequins in the window.

"That's cute," she said, rubbing a brown dress between her fingers.

She circled the clothing racks, avoiding the turned heads of other shoppers. I looked through tribal-print sweaters, neon flats, and lacy peplum tops. I imagined them on myself, but I didn't try anything on. Skye bought a flowy pair of cotton pants, a crop top, and the brown dress. All for twenty-eight dollars.

"I can't really wear these until spring, but it's good to get them now, you know?" She pushed the plastic bag up her forearm. "I still want some jewelry. Some of those feather earrings that aren't really feather? Like the metal ones?"

I nodded.

"Want to get lunch?" she asked.

There were lines at every restaurant in the food court. I looked at my phone. We had already been at the mall for an hour.

Skye followed the dominant smell to the Chinese food place. It was rich, like something decaying, but still pleasant. I bought a cinnamon roll next door. The only open seats were near the bathrooms, at a sticky table with wrinkled napkins beneath it.

"So that guy," Skye smiled with a wad of food in her cheek. "That really hot guy I told you about? I hung out with him over the break."

"You did?"

"Yeah, and we went out to this party, and we smoked and did some shots and stuff, you know, and then we came back to my place. I can't believe I ever doubted him. He's just so hot, and, I know that shouldn't be it, but I just couldn't date a guy I didn't find attractive. There has to be that physical connection. You know?"

I never knew Conner's grandfather but I kept thinking about him. Conner probably looked like him. I just imagined this long-limbed body, with white arm-hair and Conner's face, sitting in a rocking chair. Conner kind of had an old-man face already. He would fit in very well with shadows on half his face, yellow lantern-light on the other.

"And then, I mean, he's also really *smart*. He's a chemistry major. Finally, someone I meet who *isn't* a music major."

Conner really didn't seem like he would play piano. Especially not classical piano. He should walk through the mist, through the conifer mazes high in the hills. He should have soil on his boots at all times.

Skye didn't look much like a violinist, either. Or she at least looked like she would play folk songs at the farmer's market, wearing a shawl and a peasant blouse, with a headband over her wild hair.

"I could really see this going somewhere," she said.

"Yeah?"

"Yeah. Oh, oh, oh. Hey. What about that guy you were talking about?" Skye bit the straw of her soda.

I finished chewing the cinnamon roll, which clung to my teeth like clay.

"I don't know what you're talking about," I said, rubbing my hands to alleviate the stickiness. "There is no guy. I never said anything."

We threw our plates in the trash. Skye continued to sip from her plastic cup. After each gulp she pressed her lips together and made a sighing noise.

For the rest of the afternoon we walked in and out of stores. The people we passed by seemed blank and empty. There wasn't much of a difference between them and the mannequins.

As we trudged over the parking lot, I looked to the bushes lining the concrete. I watched the sky dyeing itself purple, the long grass in the drainage pond behind the dumpster.

I wondered what the mall and the parking lot had looked like before. Was it a meadow? A dry forest? What life had walked over it, and burrowed into its shoulder?

The leather seats of Skye's car bit through my jeans, chilling my thighs. We closed the doors and sealed off the wind, exchanging one car smell for another. The back seat was filled with her bags.

Skye dropped me off. I thought of going to the practice rooms. But after the lesson I'd had with Caroline that morning, I sat on the kitchen floor and ate a piece of bread instead.

"It's a new term. Let's talk. What are your goals?" she had asked me. We each ruled over a piano, our posture tall, our hands in our laps. "Your long-term goals? Where do you want to go with this?"

"I want to be a concert pianist. Or maybe teach. And I want to compose."

She pulled her thin lips up into a smile. The room smelled like her perfume; a bouquet of dried flowers. My whole nose itched with it, even the little hairs in my nostrils.

"Isn't that how we all start out," she laughed curtly. "Bright-eyed and optimistic. Then reality sets in. Then the bills come along.

"Teaching is good, though. Yeah, teaching is good. I need to be really honest with you. There aren't many people who make it beyond that. Maybe movie industry work. *Maybe.* Maybe some small gigs at a hotel or a restaurant. No one really makes their living as a concert pianist."

I looked at her in silence, smiling without teeth because I didn't know what else to do.

"Trust me, I used to have the same dream," she said.

Each time I saw Caroline she appeared closer to the ceiling. Her eyes were lined, that day, with thin, brown circles.

"Didn't you used to perform?"

"I did some recitals around. I played with an orchestra a few times," Caroline said, twirling a bangle around her pale wrist. "But I made more money teaching, and it came to the point where I didn't have enough time to do both. But, hey, I like teaching . . ."

She bit her lip.

"Okay," she said. "Let's get to work."

Why would she have told me any of that if she thought I could make it?

The first few weeks of the term were dry. As the thirsty soil drank away the snow, I practiced playing scales so fast and fluid that they, too, disappeared. Caroline told me what to play, and I played it.

I was also taking a music composition course. By the second week we moved past the basics of theory. I handed in the first assignment—to write out three measures of our own creation—a whole class period early, with an extra measure to complete the phrasing as I had heard it in my head.

When the professor handed it back, it was marked with an A- and nothing else.

That was when I lost it. That was when I walked to the park at night, all alone, with the moon in my hair. I saw the shrubs as dancing people, and I heard the wind as clarinets. My cheeks blistered in the cold. I giggled to myself with my chin pushed down to my chest. A few cars passed me on the walk over. For some reason I worried my parents were inside them, that they would see me.

Everything was dead at the park. The oak tree rattled. The sky brought me the scent of coming snow. The grass crunched with crystallized dirt.

I wasn't surprised to see Conner there. Not with the moon like liquid above the clouds.

"Are you looking for the moon, too?" he asked, wrapping his arms around my stomach from behind. He smelled like coffee beans before the bag is opened.

"You don't even surprise me anymore. Just showing up everywhere. I needed to get out."

"And this is it," he said. "This is out. At least we know the stars are back there."

We swayed with the wind for a moment, watching the

clouds turn brown around the moonlight. His arms were bare again.

"I'm getting really tired of everything, too."

"Sometimes I think I could go live for myself in the forest. Sometimes I think I don't need any of them. I don't want them looking anymore." He coughed. "I could do it."

"So why not?"

"Why not. I'm running out of reasons. There's no piano out there."

His breath was warm on my ear. I leaned back into his chest.

"We could do it," I said. "We could just run away."

"We could. Sometimes I wonder what it's all for. I was thinking about it earlier. About sea cucumbers. They just sit on the bottom of the ocean and suck up waste. That's all they do their entire lives. They don't even have sex—they just shoot out their eggs. They can't think. They don't have a brain. What are their lives for?"

"There'd be too much waste left over without them, I guess. That's their purpose. But they don't know that. They don't think. Sometimes I wonder where our thoughts come from. I wonder whether they're inside of us or not."

"Where else would they be?" he asked, running my hand over his.

"I don't know. Up behind the sky somewhere, being breathed into us by some . . . creator or something."

"Are you religious?"

"No, not really. We went to church a few times when I was little. We'd always go when my grandparents were visiting. Are you?"

"No. I was raised Christian. My parents are still avid church-goers, they go every Sunday, but I never connected with it. So are you atheist, then?"

"No. I might believe in God and Jesus and all that, but I don't know if I agree with everything about the religion. I don't know. I don't know what I am. Are you an atheist?"

"No."

"Then what do you believe in?"

"This," he said softly, like he was trying not to wake the sky from its stillness.

# Chapter Twenty

He made me feel like I could no longer sit and stare at the worlds within my own head, because they were blurry compared to the wind. He made me feel mobile. I could no longer wade in the dark corners of my apartment without imagining him there, too. Ugliness and listlessness and steadiness, and I was losing track of who I was. Something moved that had been there all along. Something crouched in the bushes, hidden within the deep threads of the ferns.

We walked together in the blue direction of the hills. Our hands worked together, swinging in union even as our steps strayed. The earth was rocky again. My eyes covered the landscape, the swinging shadows beneath the juniper trees, the red-winged blackbirds rocking back and forth on the cattails along the ditch. They dipped with the breeze's rhythm. The bright red patch of their feathers made me stop and watch.

For a moment the two of us smiled with the birds. The sun colored our fingertips, still fragile from winter. Because the day was clear we could see the mountain. It lifted up the horizon and wept white tears over it. We knew it continued along the other side, to the coast, to the world's waters, but we couldn't see the snow melting.

"It's too far now without your car," I spoke. "We can't go on any more hikes."

Conner glanced at me, then back at the unseen forests.

"I'll walk through it soon enough."

"You're really going to?"

"Camp along the way. Walk about twenty miles each day. It shouldn't take more than a week. It's not like I have any reason to rush home anyway."

"I guess. Or you could hitchhike."

"No," he said. "You can't feel anything when you're in a car."

"I wish I could go too. My parents would kill me. I do want to go hiking again before school's out, though. I want to see the wildflowers. Maybe Skye will drive us sometime . . ."

I sat next to Skye in the front seat while Conner knelt in the back. His seatbelt was off and he was turned toward the trunk, watching an elk we had just passed. The back of his neck was soft and wrinkled. He fell into his seat with a straight face, sniffing through his bony nostrils.

Skye turned the radio to another satellite station, this one featuring sporadic drumming and a repetitive melody.

"Turn it back to the classical station," I said, smiling until my eyes stretched into slits. I realized how tired I was. Most of my spring term had been spent preparing for the end of the year performance. It was only three weeks away. Caroline was finally letting me play *Fantasie Impromptu*. We needed something big, she had said, to show everyone how much I had learned. I didn't mention that I already knew the piece before I had started taking lessons with her.

If anything, she was holding me back from progressing on to more difficult works. At least I would have a different teacher the next year.

"We need to switch it up," Skye yelled over the open window. "We spend all our time listening to classical music. Playing classical music. Writing classical music. There's other stuff out there, you know. Expand your horizons, dude."

I watched the clock on the dashboard of the car. The numbers were simultaneously bright and black, flat and contoured, static and rushing. It was almost eleven. My knees felt stiff. I looked at Skye, at the fat bun on the back of her head and the way it flattened against the headrest. She paid more attention to the radio than the windshield. There was no eye shadow beneath her sharp brows, and freckles showered the bridge of her nose.

Conner squeezed the seat-belt's square ribbon in his palm. His gaze bounced between the window and the rearview mirror, where he watched Skye's picture swaying and connected his blue eyes with mine. I thought back to the hike the two of them had gone on together at the beginning of the year. What had that car ride been like?

Skye still didn't know Conner and I were together. We abstained from declaring our affection in any official terms, even between ourselves, and yet we were certainly more than friends. Neither of us was looking for other people to date. We were a couple in all ways except the title. Skye and my parents knew that we spent a lot of time together. Hallie was the only one who knew the truth.

"Okay, guys, which trailhead do you want to go to? I went on this one a few weeks ago with Marcella and we did some trail running on it." She stopped the car right there on the highway. We were alone, next to a dirt parking lot. "We could do the other one if we're just hiking, though. I mean, it's not like we care if it's rocky, right?"

We drove to the dirt parking lot a mile down. The car doors cracked. Then there was stretching, another car on the highway, and, finally, just birds. Just a song sparrow, so clear from the treetops that it sounded like it was murmuring in my ear.

Skye crouched to re-tie her lightweight, ankle-supporting hiking shoes.

"I buy new ones every season," she said. "The soles just get nasty so quickly, you know?"

As we waited I stretched my ankle in a circle, analyzing my own muddy hiking boots. Conner glanced at his worn sneakers. Besides his teva sandals, they were the only shoes he owned.

Along the trail we became a triangle—Skye in front, her footsteps sawing against the decaying leaves, and the mushrooms, and the centipedes. Her voice continually flowed until it became a weak, nasal echo against the tree bark. Conner watched the earth rolling underneath him. I looked to the flowering bushes—salal, currants, rhododendrons—that held drops of water on their petals. Each drop was small enough to be a tear, but together they distorted the colors until they glowed.

It was a still day, without much wind. The forest stood before us, and if it weren't for the dusty, sculpted path, it would have seemed infinite. Fresh waterleaf graced every dip in the landscape. The sword ferns shot straight up, not old enough to weep. Their relatives turned brown and crisp on the trees. They would trade places the next fall.

"Do you guys really want to stay on the trail all day?" Conner asked. He stopped to greet the blackened remains of a Trillium flower.

"Yeah," she snorted. "What else would we do? Get lost?"

"Just being out there doesn't make you lost. Not if you know the land," Conner said as he stood.

"Oh? And you know the landscape? How many times have you even *been* here?"

"As long as you know which direction you came from. As long as you can recognize landmarks for what they are and not just, oh, there's another tree. It's about connecting with the Earth. It's about trust."

"What, are you part Indian or something?"

"Why would that matter? Everyone's ancestors connected with the land, and with nature. For some people it was longer ago, but that doesn't mean it doesn't count. That doesn't mean we can't get back to that."

"Holy shit. I was just kidding." She pulled her arm over her chest to stretch it. Then she unzipped her fitted fleece jacket and stuffed it in her daypack. "Hey, I do my part, man. I recycle. I buy almost everything green. These socks are made out of bamboo."

No one said anything. I breathed in, shifting my

weight. Skye clipped the backpack buckle around her hips. Conner stared heavily at a fallen log. It was green with moss, red with decay, and gray with mushrooms. I could smell it even from a distance. I knew very well how it would feel to scoop up the pellets of wood, to dig through it and smell the dampness of sap. There were always those tiny yellow spheres in dirt like that. What they were, I had never known for sure. Probably some kind of bug egg.

I had always been wary of keeping bugs as pets because I knew they would die. But one day, in elementary school, I found a snail with black and white and yellow on its shell. I stabbed holes in the lid of a food container, filled it with dirt, and placed it inside. Each day I slipped in maple leaves, and some sticks to climb on. The snail left amber tracks of slime along the walls of the container. I would always find it clinging to the lid, desperate to escape.

One afternoon I came home from school and the snail was curled up in its shell. It was a sad and boring way to die, in the corner of a plastic rectangle, with the winter sun reflecting off it. I buried it in my nest of trees, with a little stick as the grave marker. When I poured out the dirt from its cage, a cluster of translucent spheres fell out. Snail eggs . . .

"What do you think we should do, May? On-trail or off-trail?" Skye asked.

"Off-trail."

"Okay," she said curtly. "Lead the way."

Fallen sticks snapped. Conner and I looped around them, but Skye broke each one in half. We followed the empty side of the sky, barely glimpsable through the fir and hemlock giants.

Conner paused in front of a Douglas fir's fat trunk. He reached out as if to touch it, but his hand only hovered over the coarse bark.

"You're so old," he muttered to it.

All three of us traced the tree from roots to canopy. The first breeze of the morning pulled through, rocking the distant leaves. The needles took shape in the way they interrupted the sky. Spring didn't forget about the evergreen trees; the tips of their branches made stripes against the dark, old foliage.

The longer I watched the tree, the more enormous it looked.

Into my head came the bobcat, and with it arrived a certain melody inherent to its presence. There was something different about it, though. Something forlorn and composed of slow-moving honey.

"It's expensive being sustainable. These socks cost thirty dollars," Skye announced as she continued walking. She broke us from our trance. Velvet Thimbleberry leaves brushed against her legging-covered calves. "And you know what I realized the other day? We're never gonna make any money. Not really. Classically trained musicians? Come on. And then I was thinking, why did I choose to major in violin? Why? Because I have no idea what else I would do, or because I love it so much that I can't imagine doing anything else?"

Our pace was slow, especially Conner's. "There's a dead mole," he said. He clenched his lips together as he crouched to look it over. The furry body was half dissolved into the earth. Its mouth was open, sharp teeth poking out. I stepped forward, my nose turned toward an azalea bush.

"And then I think, do I even care if I make a lot of money? What if I made enough to live off of, and then I could just play violin every day? How great would that be?" Skye continued. "But then I wouldn't be able to buy half the stuff I want. Or go on vacation. I don't think I could do that."

"Just become a music teacher," I told her.

"Yeah. Yeah. They still don't make a lot though."

"You really are in the wrong line of work if you want to make a lot," Conner said.

The farther away we walked from the path, the more Skye had to say. Her timid voice carried through the branches. In response to her agitated tone, the birds fell quiet.

"Sometimes I think I should maybe just be an accountant, or a lawyer. That would be so easy. Well, not easy. But, you know. Fruitful."

We came to a patch of young hemlock trees that made a barrier of sharp needles. Conner growled, something about the greed of the logging industry, but he couldn't be heard over Skye's ramblings. The branches whipped at our bodies as we pushed through them. A long, clear scratch was left on my arm. I ran my palm over it to wipe away the dusty remnants where my skin had torn.

Conner paused, as he often did, to analyze a plant he didn't recognize. It had four purple petals arranged like a star. The leaves sprouted from the stem in clusters of three.

"Must be some kind of mustard." Conner squinted at the pale flower.

I bent down and pressed my nose to it.

"It doesn't smell like anything," I said.

A woodpecker shouted its trembling laugh above us. Then there was the silence of the ancient trees.

"Where's Skye?" I bit my lip.

Conner blinked. His tired eyes turned in every direction. He scanned the floor of fallen needles, the vine maples clinging to the sunlight, the broken chunks of bark next to a downed tree.

"Conner!"

"How did she get away so quickly? Didn't she notice we stopped?"

"She's gonna freak out." I hurried back toward the young hemlocks, my back bent toward the soil in search of footprints. "She won't know how to get back by herself. Track her down, come on."

"I'm not a tracker," Conner said.

"But aren't you . . . haven't you hunted? Hunt her down, pretend she's an animal."

"She is an animal."

"So, come on!" I imagined Skye pumping her arms, swearing loudly as though we were still behind her. "You want to live in the woods, you need to know how to track."

On his face I could see he was broken; he had shattered. There was no reason for it, no pressure worthy of it, and yet it had happened. His mouth flattened into a shallow creek. He pinched the bridge of his crooked nose as he sighed.

"No footprints?" His voice cracked, almost inaudibly.

"None. I don't see any broken branches to follow. Should we just pick a direction and start walking? She couldn't have gotten far."

"Skye!" Conner yelled gruffly with his hands cupped around his lips.

I had never heard him raise his voice, let alone scream. It seemed forced from his lungs, gritty and exhausting. I cleared my throat and joined him in the calls.

It wasn't that Skye couldn't take care of herself. She was independent. She was clever. She was seductive. But she didn't know the forest. She may have grown up nearby, but she didn't know it and she didn't love it.

She could be lost in the place that Conner called home. In the forest, she was a child. I was little more than a young teenager. And Conner . . . Conner was an old man.

We yelled until our voices died. We tripped over exposed roots and fallen branches as our eyes caught the distant shade beyond the fir trunks. Dirt gripped our calves, our wrists. The yellow dust of mid-afternoon spread around us. It washed clean the smells of morning that had been hanging coolly in the air.

Our footsteps carried us in straight lines, there and back to the little firs. We invented new directions between the points of the compass. There and back, as far as we dared, over and over. My underarms leaked onto my tank-top with the constant, frantic motion.

"Does she know to stay in one place?" Conner asked.

"She's probably been walking this whole time. And talking to herself."

The day grew less beautiful. Mosquitoes surfaced, and they darted around my nose like they were determined to decorate my face with blemishes. My socks filled with scraps of wood and bark. I itched my ankle.

"Conner," I pleaded, and that was all I needed to say. I slapped a vibrating mass of flies away from my shoulders.

He held his arms calmly, loosely, at his sides, even though I could see the mosquitoes circling his knuckles.

"She has to be somewhere," he said quietly. There was a puff of moss in his hair. I dragged on his hand to stop his pace, and I reached up to pull it out.

"We'll have to go get help," I sighed.

He nodded. We made our way back to the little trees. Sitting cross-legged at their feet was Skye. Her cheeks were red and her breath was heavy. There was a streak of dirt on her forehead.

"*There* you guys are. What took you so long?" she kept her voice serious, but her eyebrows flew upward, and her chest heaved with breath.

Conner and I stared. I was afraid to move closer, as though she were a ghost.

"I don't know about you guys," she said, "but I could really use a drink."

# Chapter Twenty-One

"Sucks, you know. Sucks that I can't be in two places at once. Sucks that I'm not going to graduate in time. I switched degrees last year, and this one is so *particular*." Skye's roommate was a tall, blocky girl. Outside of class she spent all her time in her room, with tapestries arranged over the windows. Supposedly she meditated, under heavy breath, for two hours every afternoon, her palms full of sacred crystals painted black to match her fingernails. She and Skye had endured one year of high school together.

"I changed my major, too," Conner said. "Last year."

"You did?" I widened my eyes at him. We were all sitting on Skye's rough, orange couch. A coffee table made of driftwood sat in front. We rested our feet on it, with beer bottles in our hands.

"I was going to major in ecology, at first," he said quietly. He picked at the beer's label, a brightly painted waterfall. "I thought I might *minor* in music. Then I realized I liked those music courses a lot better than the ecology ones. So I switched."

"So that's why you're in a bunch of freshman classes with us, even though you're a junior," Skye laughed. She gripped her bottle from its mouth, and with it dangling in her grasp she walked to the kitchen for another. Her roommate followed. The wood floors bounced beneath her gait.

"So you never looked in to more prestigious music schools? You didn't even know you were going to be a piano major?"

"More prestigious schools? I'm happy I'm even here. Going to any college already puts me way ahead of anyone's expectations."

"Isn't it weird how this is the best school for music? You'd think it would be off in the city somewhere. I guess the openness is better for music."

Conner blew air sharply out of his nose, and he set his empty bottle next to two other ones on the floor.

"I used to hate being poor," he said. "Do you hate it?"

"I'm not poor."

"What do your parents do, again?"

"My dad's an accountant, and my mom works at supermarket part-time. And we sell fruit from our orchard in the summer. They don't make *a lot*, but we're not *impoverished* or anything."

"I am. My parents are dirt poor. But I realized that money doesn't really mean anything. So I stopped feeling bad about it. I had plenty of other things to feel bad about."

Skye and her roommate came back in, and they handed us each another beer. We talked in choppy, sputtering tones for the next hour or so. The roommate retreated to her room, and Skye went with her to smoke some weed.

"You guys feel free to stay as long as you want, stay over, whatever," she said. "If you want a smoke just come on in."

With his arm around my shoulder and his thigh against my leg, Conner said, "I can't tell you how many times I've wished for this."

"For what?"

"For a girl. For a girlfriend. For a girl like you."

I was silent. I curled my lips together because it didn't surprise me. I had certainly assumed that I was Conner's first relationship.

"You mean you've never had one? A girlfriend?"

"No. I've had some small things, but, but, none of them could look past this, in the end." He gestured to his face with his hand flat. "There was a time when I couldn't, either. I don't think anyone knows how hard it is to get to that point, where you look in the mirror and you realize, *I'm never going to grow out of this. This is not puberty, this is not temporary. This is how I'm going to look forever.* And then it gets harder to look in the mirror, and you start to wonder how other people are so lucky. And then, it's just, you look at people and you know it's harder for them to like you, just because of what they're looking at. They don't always mean it, but it happens."

"The longer I look at you, the more times I see you, the better you look. To me. You're a good height, you're not scrawny. You have a distinct face, that's all."

"Even you called me ugly that one time. When we were in the forest. You don't have to lie. Just because you don't think I'm good looking doesn't mean you can't like me."

"I guess that's all that matters, then," I said. "That I like you."

"Sometimes I wish you weren't so beautiful, so that we'd be a little more equal." He kissed me. It was slow, soft, so very kind. I felt that I was a fragile treasure in his arms and he was afraid to break me.

"Money, looks, who needs them," I said. "Let's go live in the woods."

There was a keyboard in the corner; a little electronic toy that shook when you played it. I turned it on and pushed down a plastic key. Conner stood beside me, and we played some chords with our wrists uncomfortably high. He started beating out a waltz. I improvised the melody, high in the reaches of the keyboard's treble clef. The sound that came out was dry and flat, artificially void of any ringing.

Skye popped her head out of the room down the hallway. Her eyes were red and raw.

"Shh, guys, shh, we're listening for the spirits," she whispered hoarsely before disappearing.

I pressed the off button. Two beers were in my stomach, and they pressed out against my belly button. My forehead felt hot and tired. There were still flecks of bark stuck to my wool socks. Conner looked as he always did; not unkempt, but slightly wild. His hair was approaching his neck, but he had shaved his beard. There was a pale line where his skin had been hidden beneath the hair.

"Should we go?" I asked the floor, I asked the keyboard, I asked Skye down the hallway.

"It's three in the morning."

We proceeded to dance a waltz around the room. We bumped into the furniture, into the fold-up kitchen table. The music in our heads was more than enough to guide us.

And guide us it did, throughout the next few weeks, until we reached the final recital. It was optional, and the auditorium was barren except the first few rows. We had already played for the judges earlier in the term. I missed Hallie's graduation. Her ceremony had been the same day as the judging.

It was worth it, because I passed the judge's scrutiny. Caroline bowed her head, a smile flushing over her cheeks as though she were thanking some private deity for her good fortune. I tried to play *Fantasie Impromptu*, in C-sharp minor, as I imagined Chopin himself would have played it—strong, passionate, imploring, then melting into a rich nostalgia. The piece had always reminded me of a storm on the ocean, far out at sea where no land could be seen. Even the judges looked impressed, nodding and blinking slowly as they gave me their comment sheets.

It was one of those pieces where your fingers move so fast you have no choice but to memorize it, because you can't be looking at the sheet music. All attention must go to your fingers, to the way they blur with motion.

I couldn't help imagining the future, every so often. My own compositions in the hands of a young student . . . the teacher would talk about my influence on music, the way I'd changed things. It was a selfish thing to think about, I knew. I knew you weren't supposed to think that way. I'd always believed, at least secretly, that it was okay to be cocky if you had the talent to back it up. But I wasn't so sure I had the talent, anymore.

Still, the thoughts came anyway, out of a lifetime of habit. I yearned to make my living as a composer, like Beethoven, like Chopin. Performing their work was great, but it burned through me too quickly. The connection I felt with their pieces could never pierce deep enough to persist. It didn't come from me, I was not its vessel.

Conner played his nocturne at the concert. Well, not his nocturne. Chopin's. What few people were in the audience could not move, not even with the swaying motion of a deep breath, as they were struck into statues, mesmerized by his music. The color green surged over me. His soft, floating lines painted a dogwood tree in my head. I wished there were windows in the auditorium. It would have been nice to see the wind blowing behind the stage.

When my turn came I heard many coughs, many strange shudders and whispers, but as I looked out at the end to judge their boredom, I couldn't see beyond the black curtain the lights made.

Their applause wasn't as uproarious for me as it had been for Conner. It was polite and empty. Had I not been passionate? No notes were out of place. What more did they want? What more was there?

And with that question, that recital, that light feeling of loss, school was over. My first year of college had ended.

"I have to get a job next year," said Conner. We were at

his duplex, on the back porch that overlooked a little creek. It had evaporated, except for a moistness that clung to the rocks. "I'll have to take anything I can get, unfortunately. My scholarship money doesn't cover books, or food. And I want to save up. But the kind of job I could get right now . . . delivering food or waiting tables or washing dishes . . . it would kill me. So mindless. So confining. Hey. At least I'll be free this summer."

"Call me when you get home, let me know you made it," I told Conner. "Or call me if you have any reception along the way."

"I hate even having a cell phone. If it weren't for you I would just throw it away. I'd throw it off a cliff somewhere. But I guess it's safer to have one, just in case, when I'm out there." He shuffled his bare feet against the grainy wood floor. His feet were wide and square, with toughened calluses on the heel. We walked together down the steps, our hands entwined. Conner led me down into the beige, broken grass, and we stretched out over it on our backs. I could still smell the creek water, the Alder catkins that had clumped over its still reflection. It made me sad to think of the water draining each day until there wasn't enough even for the birds to sip.

It made me sad to think of Conner walking alone as the sun was just starting to set, the trees hushed into silence without wind or birds to cry for them. I imagined him peeking his head out of a debris shelter, hoping for one last glimpse of a star or two between the branches before he fell asleep. By the time he ended up across the mountains, across the valley, and up into the hills, he would be brown from dust and days of sun. There would be no room beneath his fingernails for any more dirt. He would be unaware of the ash that had blown above his eyebrows from the last night's fire, and from the night before.

"So you'll walk along the trails, or along the highway, and camp at night. And what are you going to do for food that whole time?" I asked as I squeezed his hand.

"I'll bring some packaged stuff." He cleared his throat and sat up. "But mostly I'll get wild plants and berries. The earth provides plenty enough."

"You really think that'll be enough? I know you said—"

"You know what's next to my parent's house? A national forest. I spent three weeks out there one summer with nothing. I caught fish and foraged, mostly. That's when I taught myself to build shelters, and get a fire started quickly. Knife. Flint. A metal cup for cooking. That's all I needed."

"How old were you? Your parents just let you go out there on your own?"

"Yeah. I was seventeen. They thought I'd come back the next morning, shivering and hungry. They said, 'go try it, see what happens'." Conner laughed through his nose. "They sent my brother out halfway through to come find me. He ended up staying the rest of the week."

"How old is your brother again?" I didn't know he had a brother. I had always pictured him as an only child.

Conner licked his lips and lay back down. The sky was filling with high, transparent clouds.

"He would be twenty-five by now," he said with his pale eyes reaching upward.

"Would be?" My voice came out quieter than I intended, as though all sound was caught in my teeth and refused to surface.

"Don't worry, he's not dead. As far as I know. He just . . . doesn't talk to us anymore. After he got done with high school he took off on a road trip. One of his friends said he could get him a job in California, so he stayed there. My brother called to tell us his plan, and that he was renting out some old couple's basement. My dad kept asking about the job, what if the job didn't turn out, was his friend reliable, maybe he shouldn't have left so hastily, shouldn't have spent all his savings on rent and gas. And then my brother got mad. I don't even know why. He said he had already made more of himself than my dad ever would, just by getting out of our town. My dad hung up, and that was it. He never told us what the job even was. It was probably supposed to be some acting gig. I keep expecting my brother to turn up on a commercial or something."

I didn't know what to say, so I stretched closer to him.

"Then again," he snorted, "I don't even watch TV anymore."

"Neither do I. Only when I'm at home."

He turned over on his shoulder to face me, and he cupped his hand around my chin. It was between cold and warm, wet and dry.

"Feels right, doesn't it?" he said. "Being right up against the ground? Seems like we came from there, or from the sky or something, but we came from the ocean."

His hand moved gently to my cheek. I could feel him breathing through it. A breeze brought us smoke from someone else's fire. It was too early for an evening bonfire, and far too warm to have one going in the fireplace.

"You smell that?" I asked.

"Must be wildfires off east of here. It's been dry enough."

"Wildfires? It's only June."

"Happened last year, too."

"Be careful you don't get caught in one when you're hiking over the mountains."

"That sounds powerful. Going over the mountains. But I don't want it to be, I don't want it to be me on top of the mountain. I want to always keep it in my head that the mountain is holding me up." He hummed and breathed at once. "Hmm. That is really strong." His eyes became pools of water.

I sat up. "Conner." I looked back at their duplex. A black cloud was sitting on the roof, billowing and shrugging like a wave.

We jumped up. I pulled my phone out of my pocket.

"Wait, let's go see. Maybe it's smaller than it looks," he said. "It's probably just in one room; the toaster's on fire or something."

I dialed 9-1-1 and hovered my thumb above the call button. "Don't go inside," I coughed. "It's coming out the roof. I think it's bad. Where's your roommate? He's not inside, is he?"

"What could have . . . No, no, he's off in Montana or somewhere. On vacation."

"Then is there anything valuable inside?" A flame consumed the once-gray roof. There was a deep thud, a vibrating bass, and the building began to melt away. "I'm calling."

We backed away onto the neighbor's grass. The wind passed through the fire, and my arms stood restless with goose bumps of heat. It stunk like cloth burning, like living wood when it is sacrificed into smoke. I felt like I shouldn't be looking directly at it. The house trembled and transformed into a standing lake of flame.

"I guess I'm not taking anything with me after all," Conner whispered. "I just hope I don't have to pay for this. I can't. *I can't.*"

Neighbors crept out from their homes and stood in a line on the road. Why had it taken them so long? Conner and I stayed behind the house, kneeling in the well-mown grass of his neighbor. I could see one woman dressed in a Hawaiian shirt taking a picture with her i-phone out front. The fire truck came, its siren so loud it muffled the scalding breath of the burning house. They rushed out in their heavy yellow suits, spraying the building.

I stopped looking. Instead I turned around and faced the low sun. The same wispy clouds we had been watching earlier were approaching it, ready to force an early dusk upon the land. But then it would move again. The tree line would be next, and then the hills; each would take his turn stealing the sun, until it was the ocean's turn far off where we couldn't see.

When the fire was dead and black, they came over to talk to us.

"Which half of the duplex was yours?" the man asked. He was short and skinny, with his eyebrows thin at the edges.

"The left half. If you're looking in from the street."

"Do you know the residents of the other half?"

"Sort of. It was just one guy. I talked to him when I rented the place. He owns it. But then I never really saw him again." Conner paused. "He wasn't in there, was he?"

"We did find a body, but we can't confirm whose it is, or the cause of the fire."

Conner knew. Conner knew it was him, his landlord, who had died, and his jaw hardened.

"Go get some rest," the man said when he saw Conner's pink face contort into a heavy, blank wall. "Do you have a place to stay?"

Of course I let him stay with me. We slept next to each other on my bed, I under the blankets, he on top of them, far enough apart to encourage a platonic night's rest. The bed sloped down toward him, toward his heaviness, his denseness. I listened to his shallow, ragged breathing as I stared away into the fuzzy darkness. When I woke up the next morning, he was gone.

I assumed he had started out on his walk. I assumed he was troubled, that he needed to think, that he felt some irresistible pull of freedom because he wasn't tied to any possessions. I assumed he didn't say goodbye because he was too upset, and too uncomfortable for imposing on me with nowhere else to go. Too restless to wait.

"Oh, Conner . . ." I whispered to myself.

When I went into the kitchen for breakfast, I saw the note on the table. It was written on the back of a used envelope I had placed in the recycling basket.

*May*, it read in careful, angled letters, *Thanks for letting me stay last night. I'll see you later today.*

And that was it. My parents were coming that afternoon to help me move out. I hoped he would come before they did.

I got to packing my clothes, my dishes, my bedding. As I shoved these things into cardboard tombs, my stomach began to ache with the excited happiness of being done. Done with all work, done living in the Studio; next year I would be rooming with Skye and Sandal Girl. I realized I had hated living in the Studio all along; I'd hated the low ceilings, the unexplainable dampness of the walls despite the lack of rain.

In the afternoon the door rattled.

"He killed himself," Conner said as soon as he saw my face. His eyes were so taut; they bulged horrendously from under his heavy forehead. "He started the fire. He killed himself."

"Your neighbor? Your landlord?" I covered my mouth with one hand.

"The only time I saw him was when he was taking out the trash. He didn't seem normal, but he didn't seem crazy. He was bald, and really pale, and he wore this puffy orange vest almost every day. Sometimes I heard his music through the wall. Jazz music. That was it. That was all I knew about him. And he had a cat. Cat got out, though. It was always hanging out down the road, anyway, sitting underneath this one willow tree."

"What are you going to do?" I asked. We were still in the doorway. The afternoon was growing hot. Even the wind was tepid. I motioned for him to come inside. "We can give you a ride home if you're not up to walking all that way. I mean, all your stuff is gone. You can always try it next year. I'm sure you have a lot to figure out, with insurance and everything."

"I wasn't responsible. I only need to get involved if I want reimbursement for the stuff I lost, and I don't give a shit about that. I just need a lighter, a knife, some cord, and a metal bowl. I'm going to go take some money out of my account, buy those things, and head out later today. I just came to say goodbye." He hugged me, there beneath the doorframe. I rested my ear on his warm chest. He kissed me, one hand sewn into my hair.

"Oh, and my cell phone was inside the house. It's gone. So I won't be able to call you. Maybe at home, in about a month. Whenever I get back."

I nodded because I knew there was no way I could change his mind. I knew I was doomed to a summer without him, three months of solitude. He stepped away and I smiled sadly with my lips closed. Before I had even closed the door, my parent's car pulled up to the apartment. They climbed the stairs, brightly clad in summer clothes.

"Who was that boy who was on the porch with you?" my mom asked. "Was that that boy we gave a ride to last year? Conner?"

"Yeah. Actually, we're pretty close now. We hang out a lot."

"Oh," my mom nodded. "Well he seemed like a nice boy."

We packed up the car, drove home, unpacked again. Hallie had fallen asleep on the couch, watching MTV, clutching her arms into her chest. She would stay at home until she started her new job as a middle school teacher in the fall.

My room was cloaked in unused air. I opened the windows, brushing away the dead stink bugs and centipedes on the sill.

The maple tree was pale in the moonlight, but I couldn't see the moon itself. Venus's vast, yellow light stabbed through the branches. In an hour or two it would join the moon, and the two would sit idly next to each other as bright rulers of the sky.

As the night spread, covering up all remaining blue, I wrapped my bed in fresh sheets. The air began to sting, and the leaves outside whispered fragrant words to me. Rain shook the roof. The screen in the window was stained with dark circles. I closed the glass until only a sliver of the window remained open to the outside world. That way I could still hear the rain singing.

It was odd for it to rain at night, especially in the summer. I had grown so used to the desert. There were fewer stars at home, too, than in the black desert sky. Or more light pollution, really. If it weren't for the vomit of cities, towns, freeways, skyscrapers, ugly concrete sculptures carpeting our feet, far-reaching and dominating, every piece of the sky would be graced with silver pins of light far more beautiful than anything man could create.

# Chapter Twenty-two

I just wanted to know if he was *alive*. Conner didn't call me. If we weren't together, for real, in person, he didn't exist. I had to wonder if he had made it through alright. Why hadn't I written down his home phone number? Several nights I lay awake, staring at the ceiling, contemplating taking my parent's car and driving to Conner's house.

So many things could have gone wrong. When I thought of them my eyes turned into immovable blocks; I would gaze away, seeing nothing, until I grew so angry at his selfishness that I decided not to drive over after all.

It was agony. Strange waves of thought crept over my mind. Where is the moon, I thought? Where is it when I cannot see it? Who is dominant, the earth or the moon? They cannot exist without each other. How long will it be until the moon drifts away, leaving the blue glass around the planet cracking and cracked? How long will it be before the sun swells and consumes us both? We exist knowing there will be an end to all things. Yet this seemed to bother very few people.

I tried to wake up, but I couldn't think of anything else. How do I use this within my art, I wondered, as endless shadows at the core of bright illustrations?

The birds outside called to me. I followed them to the orchard, where the sunlight was growing old. One robin sang—up in pitch, down, trill, up again. There was moss on the apple trunks where there had never been before. It was coarsely soft, and it scraped against my ankles as I climbed. My bare feet had not yet grown dark and tough. I could feel every knot in the bark, every bump.

A ruby-crowned kinglet hovered next to a small, green apple, its wings billowing like a hummingbird's. I watched it swim over the flat air and down to the grass, fluttering and twirling in energetic gusts. I stared until my eyes watered, until the bird sloped up over our house and disappeared into the fields beyond.

I stretched my legs over the branches of the apple tree. Conner came into my mind, a conversation we'd had on a walk. We were crossing a field. The one next to the park. Others would have said that weeds were taking it over.

Conner and I avoided stepping on the agoseris, the wild lettuce, the plantain, and the dock. We glanced at our feet after every few steps.

"It's so ugly," he had said when the square frames of the housing development across the street came into view. "They keep building on more land and more land. There's not going to be any left."

"What else are they supposed to do? People need somewhere to live. I guess they could live in smaller houses. Or houses on top of each other—apartments. We don't need to take up so much space."

"Would you want to live in an apartment? High up in the city, where you couldn't even touch the ground, or rush outside to see how the wind blows through the ferns? Would you want to be that separated from the earth?"

"There are too many people now for us to all go back to living sustainably, in, you know, earth-based lifestyles." I shrugged. "It's better to crowd everyone together in the city than to spread out and destroy more ecosystems for the sake of suburbs."

"So only some people get to see the sun rise and set in the open fields? Only the select few get to see how its angle changes with the seasons? Everyone else is surrounded by concrete?"

"Frankly, even if we had enough space and resources for us all to live a subsistence lifestyle, not everyone would want to."

"Because they don't know what it's like. They've spent their whole lives in captivity, thinking their welfare depends first on money and second on the planet."

"Then how can they hunger for something they don't know? Let's save it for those of us who have wildness in our blood."

"Then how will they ever learn to care? Why would they bother to change their lives, to strip away conveniences, just to protect something they know only as an abstraction?"

"Because if they refuse to do so, they die."

"You're right. Not immediately. Slowly, from poison, from suffocation, from the soil cracking beneath their feet and the concrete boiling into lava," Conner said. The sun was behind his head, making his ear glow a translucent orange. He gestured with his hand, up and down, chopping, as he spoke. "Here's the dilemma: there are two main ways to live lightly upon the land. Either cities have to be designed so you can get from place to place without driving a car, so, in other words, they have to be compact. Everything's got to be crunched together. Food has to be grown near the city, right outside of it. No room for suburbs there. Or, you can live out in the country, in the wilderness, basically, and provide for yourself. No shipments of goods, no commuting to work. You grow or catch your own food, and you pull your own water from where it runs. You only go into the city for emergencies."

"So either you go all the way, or nature is something you visit on vacation."

"The dilemma," he had said resolutely, with a shake of his head. "And we created it. It's a population problem, really. Not much we can do about it now, except change our lifestyles."

We had continued walking until we reached the park. Our park. We had eaten bearberries off their creeping vine, and smelled the scentless stink of currant flowers. Then he had pulled me into his arms, humming into my ear a strange song, like the wind when it cuts through the naked arms of trees during winter. The dirt was a rich brown. It was watered each evening by sprinklers, along with the lawns and the trees of the park. Without such interference, the trees would never have grown so dense or so tall. Without false rain, that park would've been dirt and sagebrush and juniper.

"Just because someone planted these, does that mean they don't belong here?" I stared up into the shimmering alder leaves.

"No. Like you said, we have wildness in our blood. The only thing is, it's not just us. It's every human being on the planet. Some of them just haven't realized it yet."

The clouds clustered along one edge of the sky. I couldn't decide whether I should stay out or go inside. Conner faded away, as much as he ever did, while still remaining a soft image beneath my eyelids.

My summer was full of such days. I discovered an eagle nest on the far side of the fields, by the fence. It was at the top of a fir tree; a fat circle of sticks that reminded me of hay atop a toothpick. When I tilted my chin up towards it I heard the babies slurping air into whistling chirps, but I could never see their gray heads. Sometimes the mom flew over in two great gusts. Her wings moved slowly like stagnant water. She wasn't a bald eagle, nor a golden eagle. I hadn't mistaken her for a hawk or a falcon. I tried to catch the colors of her feathers, but I only ever saw her from below. The sun saw every color, while I could see only the gray shadows beneath.

I sat at the base of the tree. My eyes studied the crevasses in the bark, searching the holes and flakes that composed its skin. I didn't know what I was looking for, or if I was even looking for anything, but I kept gazing forward and up. The dirt cut into my knee. When I stood, I noticed that my ankles had been pierced with the imprints of fir needles.

"May, come here for a second," my mom yelled from the front door.

I stepped lightly over fallen branches, trying not to let the dead leaves crunch beneath my sneakers. There was a car in the gravel driveway. It was red, small, flat; it had tear-shaped scratches beneath the windows.

"Who's here?" I asked when I saw my mom in the doorway.

She wrinkled her bony nose as a slow smile overtook her face. She parted her lips, but then another face surfaced over her shoulder. From the dimness of the entryway came an equally dim countenance. His eyebrows fell low over his light, milky eyes. He said nothing. I said even less. My mom shifted her weight to the wooden step below the door. She wiped her hands on the thighs of her jeans.

Conner stepped forward. He grabbed my hand like he was going in for a handshake, but he just held it. Our fingers and our arms were connected in a bridge between our two bodies. I looked at my mom, who licked her lips and coughed at the ground. The tips of my fingers began to sweat, and so did the back of my neck. I turned from Conner and my mom, and I walked back beneath the trees.

The sun was setting over them. It was the slow, churning dance of the wind and the clouds that in summer seemed never to end.

"I told you I'd let you know," he said from behind.

"Couldn't you have called me? It's been two months since you should've gotten back. Summer's almost over." I paused to hear the woodpecker sing from a few trees down. "I thought you were dead."

"I couldn't call you. I didn't have a phone."

"Why not?" My jaw tightened.

He circled around and stood in front of me. His skin was red, peeling along his nose.

"I dropped it. In a stream. It stopped working."

"You couldn't get another one? You couldn't call me on your home phone?" My breath came shallowly and my hands were restless.

"I forgot your number. It was programmed into my phone but I forgot it. I had your address because you sent me that Christmas card. I didn't realize it until yesterday. Sending a letter would've taken too long, after all this time. So I had to come to you."

I sat down on a mossy rock. Conner crouched next to me. He picked at the earth and ran his fingers over crunchy, brown fern fronds. "I'm not getting another phone," he said. "I don't need one."

"I thought you didn't need another car, either."

"It's my parent's. I'll only drive if there's no other way. If I had walked I wouldn't have reached you in time. You would've gone back to school. I don't have a bike. The train and bus don't come here . . ."

"You should've hitchhiked," I said. "But I guess that's still a car. You're such a perfectionist. Everything is for the earth. The earth mother. Mother earth. There are other things in life. You can't be a slave to mother earth."

"Nothing lives on this planet who isn't. We would be nothing without the air and the water and the sun, without the soil and the plants and the other animals. Don't you see that? We would be nothing without this. Don't you see that this is sacred? *We are this.*" He held up a pinch of dirt, scooped up and out of the grass by a mole hill. It dripped through the cracks between his cupped fingers. "And don't you see that it's *fulfilling* to stop worrying about buying things, using things, making money, getting places quickly; to free yourself from this eternal circle of brainwashing that they have us under, telling us more, more, more, faster, faster, be content with inequality and environmental destruction, as long as you have money and *things?*"

I looked away from him. His chin disappeared as he swallowed.

"There was no piano out there, May. There were no instruments, but there was music."

We sat next to each other, listening to the squirrels jump from branch to branch. One screeched, a vibrating yelp.

The sun cut a pathway through the branches, constructing my knee into a yellow cave of light. I rested my hand there. It trembled within the sunlight.

I never cried. I didn't know why I was crying, and neither did he. Conner stood me up, his hands in my armpits, and wrapped his arms around me. I shook along my spine and down my legs with soundless sobbing. When I pulled back, his t-shirt was wet.

"Sorry," I mumbled with my eyes closed. "God. Sorry." I rubbed at my eyelashes. I wanted them to come off along with the dampness along their edges.

Conner left, after that. He kissed me and he left. He had to go home because his dad needed the car.

"I'll see you at school," he said.

I left the sunset, so bright pink it cloaked the grass fields in red, and I sat at the piano bench. My own music was the only thing that could soothe me. So I played.

"Damn," Hallie laughed. She appeared at my side and looked down at the top of my head. "You were right about him, May. That was him, right? He's ugly as hell. But, hey, if you're into that . . ."

"Shut up. Please shut up, Hallie." I wanted to tell her that she was ugly, that her eyebrows were overgrown or her skin was blotchy. But that wouldn't have been true.

She tilted her neck so she could see my eyes as they stared straight ahead at the sheet music.

"Look," she said. "If you like him, that's all that matters."

She walked away. Her heels beat down heavily on the wood floors. Her small voice called once more from down the hallway.

"Did you know humans are evolutionarily inclined to choose mutually attractive mates?" she said.

# Chapter Twenty-three

"I want to be a composer."

"Well, play something for me, then. I'll tell you if you've got it or not—you either have it or you don't. It's one of those things. Go on." My new piano teacher motioned to the keys. "Play."

I looked down. White paint was chipping off the keys and the wood was showing. It was an old upright. My teacher, Mr. Edmondson, crossed his legs. He sat at a short grand piano on the other side of the room.

"I give the students the worse piano. That way they'll learn it's not the piano, it's the pianist. Go on, play."

I improvised something new. It had been rotating through my mind for days, but I'd been afraid to breathe life into it.

What it really was was the robin's song, carried up through the clouds until it reached the light blue dust between earth and outer space. My parents had told me about heaven, although I could tell that they didn't believe in it. I imagined heaven as the cliff at the edge of the universe. This song was the voice of the robin, sad and reaching, winding through moons and stars that human eyes would never see. I had a feeling that when the robins looked up they saw it all.

"How old are you, again?"

"Nineteen."

"Good. Good. Well that was . . . I'll be honest. I've never heard anything like it before. And when you think of all the composers that have come before you, that's honestly a hard thing to do. What kind of music do you compose?"

"Symphonies, concertos. Piano pieces, of course. It's hard, because I usually don't even write anything down. And I never get to hear it out loud, not the orchestral pieces."

"You . . . envision the piece in your *head*?"

He held up a fat, square finger. His hands were long and thick; they were the heaviest part of his body. He reminded me of a sedge along the river, thin and flat and wide. His hair was gone except around the ears, where it stuck out like wire. Even his eyebrows were bald. When he spoke he licked his lips, and his tongue made every word wet.

"Here." He reached into his leather briefcase, which was scuffed at the base. "This is the number of my friend Gertrude Meisner. Give her a call and tell her you're my student. Or, you know what, I'll call her and tell her you're going to call. She's the director of the youth orchestra in town. She was just asking me the other day for some new material. Something along these lines would be perfect. Modern but still reflective of the romantic era. It would get great publicity, performing a student work."

I stared at the black and white photo on the wall of an oak tree with the sun behind it. My eyes were unable to move. My mouth was frozen.

"Your music is complex," Mr. Edmondson went on. He smiled. "It's strange, but it has power behind it. With a little fine-tuning, you could really make something of yourself. And your playing—it's . . . it's phenomenal. Excellent. Excellent technique."

"Thanks. Thank you." I felt like I should say something more, but I was incapable of it. For the rest of the day I walked around in stunned silence. Had my music improved that much, or was Edmondson just less picky? I didn't care. Either way, he liked it. Either way, my music was alive. It was what I had secretly, eternally been wishing for.

I walked to the apartment Skye and I shared with Sandal Girl. It was right across the street from the music building. I turned the plastic doorknob. The beige carpet was sandy from someone else's shoes. Chunks of dirt and grass littered the loops of fabric, but I didn't care. Nor did I care that the walls smelled like weed, or that the table I'd bought for the living room had a puddle of brown liquid on it, or that the only room with a window was the kitchen. I pulled out my phone and crouched in the corner.

"I already have a few possibilities, a few people who've tried out. But come on in, I'll hear you," Gertrude said in a kind, raspy voice.

The next week I auditioned at the concert hall. She wanted to hear my playing as well as see the sheet music. I had spent all weekend writing out a new piece. Gertrude looked it over, turning the flimsy pages of my notebook with manicured fingernails.

"Great. I'll let you know," she said with a nod.

I stepped over the black carpet of the hall, careful to tread light enough so the echoes of my feet wouldn't drown out the lingering vibrations of my music. The red seats were empty, but I could imagine them full and rapt. My chest was full. I blinked slowly as the overcast sky replaced the golden ceiling.

A week went by. I thought back to the way her round face had looked, with wrinkles at the edges of her eyes. I had watched her out of the corner of my eye as I played piano.

She wore a black suit, fitted around the waist, with quarter-length sleeves and a golden watch. Was she impressed? She wasn't as complimentary as Edmondson, but was she even *allowed* to be? It was an audition, after all. She had to be fair to the others. The look on her face was calm and blank.

Then she finally called.

"I'm sorry. Not this time."

When the phone clicked into deadness I bit my lip. I knelt in front of my bed and rested my chin against the mattress.

"Where's my backpack," I mumbled. I found it underneath a chair in the kitchen. I stuffed warm clothes, a water bottle, my wallet, my phone, and a granola bar inside it.

Then there was fresh wind upon my cheeks, fragrant of nothing but asphalt and the dumpster in the alley next to our building. I coughed until my breath made a cloud of morning fog in front of my nose. The road was empty, but I walked hopefully along the black path with my thumb sticking up. I hoped Skye couldn't see me from the apartment, although I was sure she had gotten drunk enough the night before to sleep in for a few more hours. And she would have to be standing in the kitchen, at the sink, squinting out the rectangle of glass, to see anything but the dark green wallpaper.

The morning was cold but I knew it would warm up. I walked for miles. My old sneakers rubbed against my ankles. I was wearing running shorts and a thin sweatshirt. The edge of the wind raised bumps on my skin, but walking kept me from shivering.

Cars drove past and I hated them. I could tell they hated me too by the way they swerved angrily to the other side of the street to avoid me, and then sped up with a roar.

Finally a silver truck pulled over and rolled the window down.

"Where you headed?" a bearded man yelled over the passenger seat, one hand on the steering wheel, the other cupped over his mouth.

"West," I said. "Toward the mountains."

"Alright. Hop on in, I'll take ya."

The seats were covered in thick, wool blankets. It smelled like cigarette smoke. The man clicked off the radio, which had been turned to a country station. He cleared his throat. When he spoke his pale forehead wrinkled. He asked me my name, my age, where I went to school.

"And my name's Henry, by the way," he replied. "My wife calls me Albert sometimes. I think she thinks I'm her brother. She has Alzheimer's, you see, really early onset. She's only in her late forties. My mother-in-law lives at home with us, takes care of her during the day. I work out with the timber companies. I don't do the cutting, but I do the behind the scenes stuff. Sit at a desk, you know. Yeah. It's rough, alright, my wife being the way she is. She won't sleep with her brother, that'd be incest." He chuckled.

I coaxed a hesitant laugh in response, a dip of my throat that sounded like I was swallowing. My backpack rested on my thighs. I crossed my legs beneath it and looked out the window.

Henry started to whistle. It was upbeat and creepy. I pulled my phone from my bag and held it in my hand for comfort. If he tried anything, I'd be ready.

As the hills changed from brown to green, I realized my phone had lost reception.

"You're a pretty one," Henry said with a smile. His teeth were brown along the gum line.

"Thanks," I mumbled. The car stopped. The beer cans in the backseat shot forward.

"Where exactly you headed? This far enough? We're about to the pass."

"Yeah. Yes, thank you so much." I swung my legs out the door.

"Need me to pick you up some time later?" he asked. His voice was soft and gruff. "I come by this way on my drive home."

"No thanks. Thank you for the ride, though. Bye, Henry." And I walked quickly into the cover of the trees.

I needed the comfort of the woods, but without Conner, without Skye, and certainly without Henry. I didn't want to tell anyone about my failure, especially not Conner. He fell in love with me because of my compositions. I didn't want him to change his mind.

And I wanted to be alone. Really, truly, alone, except for the living beings of the forest. I walked until I couldn't see the road anymore. Then I dropped my backpack and I sat at the base of a hazelnut tree. I grabbed one of its velvet, serrated leaves from a low branch. As I listened to the chickadees and the jays, I tore it carefully apart.

The wind was absent but the trees still seemed to move. All the trees around me were red cedar, except for the hazelnut and some yew in the understory. Red huckleberry bushes were full and ripe, and snowberry dotted the dusty hill. I closed my eyes as Conner often did. When I asked him why he did that, he said he was feeling the forest, all the life around him. He said it was his way of acknowledging their presence.

I was beginning to understand who "they" were, but I still knew very little about what Conner himself had taught himself. I couldn't walk through the forest without fear of losing my way. I couldn't make a fire with a bow, or even flint. I couldn't find wild plants to eat, or catch a fish with my bare hands; nor could I make a rainproof shelter, or use the stars to guide myself home.

Ants infested my leg, so I stepped away. They clung to my skin until I brushed them off. I found, behind the cedar grove, a field of bunchberry and anemones, their white flowers glowing against the mossy dirt. As I walked I sang to them.

Time circled around me. I called it the sun and walked on. Drip, drip, drip came the light of afternoon; came the shifting breeze of dusk. I nodded to the trees with secret words of thanks that I hid behind my eyes. By the time I reached the highway my underarms were sweating. I crossed my legs beneath me and waited for a car to take me home.

The robin bellowed his high, evening alarms. Still no cars, none that would stop at the request of my thumb. I headed back into the forest. Bracken ferns swayed against my calves. A breeze stirred amber orbs of cottonwood fluff until they coated the dirt in a fuzzy lining. I followed the wind to its origin, the banks of a delicate stream that flowed so slowly it was a perfect mirror.

I changed into the sweatpants and jacket I had brought. It felt strange to change out in the open, like someone could see my tight, pale stomach, so I left my bra on and hunched my shoulders over. Then I squatted next to the water. Would the churning echo of the stream cease at dusk? It seemed there could be nothing after the sun went away.

In the muddy sand along the water I saw an imprint. As I bent closer, I recognized the wide toes; the round paws. Conner had pointed it out to me before. It was a bobcat, and the tracks were fresh.

There was no need to run, but I did so anyway. I jogged through spider webs, stumbling over stumps and ant mounds, until I was back at the grove of cedar trees. With restless hands I picked salal berries, huckleberries, and blackberries to eat along with my granola bar. My fingers were left a dark purple.

A crack sounded, and I jumped up. It was only a finch perched on an elderberry bush.

"Bobcats need to eat," I mumbled. The finch darted away. "We kill to eat. Everything. Everything relies on death to survive, except plants. Lucky plants."

My voice dispersed and it was silent besides my chewing. My eyes throbbed with tired dryness, but I was shaking too steadily from the cold to fall asleep. I could feel the earth growing frigid beneath my legs. I tried to bunch some ferns together to sit on, but I could still feel the sharp bite underneath. It was too late to make a shelter. The sun was gone.

I found myself counting the things I missed; heat, warmth, a hot shower, a heavy meal. The sun. Without Conner the woods were less benevolent. I wanted to light a flashlight or a fire so I could see what was around me. My phone screen provided a pale glow.

Numbness settled over me. I suppose I was in a trance, imposed by hunger and by near-hypothermia. A cackling, gurgling noise lit the air behind me. It was an alien squeal, a broad and bitter waterfall. There was a bobcat behind me. I was sure of it. All I could do was hum, and rub together the clammy palms of my hands. My phone was running out of power.

In such helplessness I wondered if I should pray to someone. I chose the moon to pray to. It was above the canopy, out of sight, but I knew it was there. A half moon. It would be glorious and steel blue, shining in a feathery wash upon the tops of the ancient trees. Late in the night a shadow reached me. The moon left my hands long and black. I prayed continuously—not with my palms pressed together, but by gazing up at the sky, or at wind in silent branches.

In life, in the energy of being, there is something one can't explain. It's what makes you alive. I realized, then, that I believed in something. A god who was in all things living, who was the sky but not angels.

Maybe I didn't know how to survive in the wilderness, but I knew how to love it. And that was more than most people could say.

By the time the first birds sang I was walking. The road was foggy, and it smelt like fake leather. Dew had made it wet. My pants were soaked up to the thigh from rubbing against damp leaves.

A car stopped for me when the sun was in the south. I felt dirty after only one night; I was sure my features were clouded with dust, and that there were felty, oval leaves in my hair.

It was a woman who stopped for me. She drove an SUV with a sticker on the window that said *I'm a hybrid! Learn more at www.gogreen.org*. She wore a crude beaded necklace that looked like a child had made it.

"You look like you need a ride, you poor thing." She pursed her lips as her eyes dropped to my muddy sneakers. "I'm headed into town."

I thanked her with a worn voice. Her seats were leather and the heat was turned up to a stuffy level. It was a tragedy that anything so luxurious existed.

No music played. The car stunk of coffee. Her necklace was, without a doubt, a child's handiwork.

"Were you . . . camping?" she asked. Her voice was whiny, and carried the inflection of someone who asks for favors often.

"Yeah."

"It was cold last night. How was it, camping out?"

"It was cold," I laughed.

We rode the rest of the way without words. When she dropped me off at the school, I was still so tired that I was emotionless. The emptiness also came from knowing that, without Conner, I couldn't walk the great forestlands; I couldn't yet find peace in the way the blue sky traced the clouds, no matter how much I loved it.

# Chapter Twenty-four

Conner and I climbed the oak tree again. We lounged on the thick, rough branches, one on top of the other.

"You're graduating soon," I said without looking at him. "This weekend."

He said nothing in return. I glanced at the top of his head; at the messy river of a part that ran through his brown hair. It was more like fur than hair.

"I don't know how you did it so quickly, switching majors," I went on.

"I had all the general requirements out of the way, so I had time to get the music stuff done."

The day was smothered in low clouds. Every so often I felt a needle of mist brush against my nose. The birds rustled occasionally in the flowering bushes below, off and on, the leaves shaking in great bursts of blue light. Conner watched them. His legs were bent up to his chest. They looked rosy and surprisingly hairless in the shade.

He slid his hands against the bark and sighed.

"I'm going to Europe. I'm leaving on Monday."

"Oh my god . . . well, good, that'll be fun. When will you be back?" Why didn't he tell me sooner?

A pause. "I'm going with hardly anything. Just a backpack. Then I'm going to take the train around. I've been saving up money for years. *Years.* Since high school. I want to see the mountains, the great steppes, the Mediterranean. I want to cut down into Morocco and taste the desert air. I might even go farther east, to Asia or the South Pacific."

"So, what, a few months?"

"I have no schedule. I want to be a traveler. I want to be weightless, May." He turned his dull, heavy eyes up to me. "I want to work temporary jobs as I go, actually *live* in the places I travel to, get to know the locals."

"I understand. Don't worry, I'll be here for you. However long—"

"I can't ask that of you. We both need our freedom."

"But . . . I don't want it."

"But I do."

"Come on. You're being selfish. Can't you go without breaking up with me?"

"We're both being selfish. This is good for both of us. We need to walk on our own for now. We need to grow."

"Stop. You're so selfish," I cried. "You want to go off on your adventures and leave me here. Why can't you just give me that reassurance, that promise that you'll come back and we'll be together again? Is that too much to ask? No one else will want you, you know. No one else will be like me, no one else will be like you . . . . You know that already, but you still want to look? You've been dying for an escape, haven't you?"

"No, no. I just want to see what there is to the world. Life is so short. I want to find myself."

"*Find* yourself? How cliché can you get? The only people who say those kinds of things are the people who aren't satisfied with themselves in the first place. You know yourself, how can you not? You *are* yourself. What you really want is to change."

"May—"

"No. Fine. Whatever. I have to go." I pinched the sides of my eyes along the bridge of my nose. Then I slid down the tree trunk.

"May, wait, hold on . . . "

But he didn't come down from the oak tree. He sat in its arms and I felt his eyes on my back.

# Chapter Twenty-five

Who could I tell about his flight to Europe? Who could I tell about the hole in my stomach, or about the wetness that sank into my eyes but never fell?

Skye assumed I was upset because he was my close friend.

"It's not easy being left behind." She rested her fingers on my arm, her golden-orange hair gathering in a maze upon the back of the sofa. "I know. My dad left when I was two years old."

"But I met your dad––"

"He's my stepdad, but he's still, you know, my dad in every way except genetics. And I don't even miss my birth-dad. I'm better off without him. He's an asshole. You know? Into heavy drugs and shit." She studied my face, my cheekbones and my chin, with a soft smile. "Let me know if you want to talk some more. Don't worry. I know how it feels."

"Thanks. But, um, what I really want is . . . can I borrow your car? Please, can I borrow it just for one weekend?" I swallowed roughly, heavily, my eyes slits upon the floor.

Sandal Girl sat next to Skye on the couch and dug her elbow into the back. She snorted over her phone. Her legs were pulled up underneath her, crossed sideways so her Birkenstocks dangled away from the pillows. I stood on the rug.

"I can drive you anywhere, you know. Where did you want to go?" Skye said.

"That's the thing. I . . . want to be alone."

"You can take my car," Sandal Girl shrugged.

"Really?"

"I'm not using it this weekend. Just pay for gas."

"I was going to let her take mine. I just wanted to know where she was going," I heard Skye say as I left to fill my backpack.

When I made it there I stepped out onto the soil; I clicked the car doors locked and pulled on the handle to check; I walked away from the asphalt river and toward the flowering stream. The gravity of the earth pulled me to my knees. I sifted my hands desperately into last year's fallen leaves, bowing before the trees.

He was not there. He would not be there.

Crying, crawling, dust in my eyes from rubbing the tears away. The sun was soon to die. Every brown was gold, and every green was deadened into silver. Unknown insects called; their sound was cool dusk-water.

It had been a year. A douglas fir had fallen since I had been there last. Its bark rolled off in thick chunks, exposing the pale, scurrying flesh beneath. I gathered the boards of fallen bark and piled them against their mother log. They stacked easily. It was their grooves that held them together. It was their thickness that lent warmth. I built the shelter low to the ground, with a stack of orange needles for carpet and a doorway only just large enough to slip through on my stomach.

Spiders and ants shared the ceiling with my breath. I couldn't make fire without a lighter, so I didn't make one. The air was not yet cold.

I regretted growing older. There was something sad about the way the clouds smelled like rain even though I felt how dry it was. Outside my shelter I clenched my teeth and just stood, stood and swayed and watched the ground give way to stained-glass colors. There was something I needed to do, something I needed to say, but it remained a hidden spark only the other animals could see.

If I couldn't stop Conner I could at least do this.

Over all things I heard my own breathing. I was stuck inside myself. The trees sighed. They were breathing, too.

There was a cigarette butt at the base of a tree. There were white violets next to the stream. I waded my fingers in to test the water temperature. It was shallow enough to be warm, so I threw off my hiking boots and rested my feet atop the pebbled bottom. My heels scraped against water plants; minnows fled the currents of my kicking.

The maple trees above me . . . I fell asleep there, lying on my back, as I took in the life around me. When I sat up in the early night my feet were pink blisters and my arms were spotted. I shook each foot to dry it off before I tried to force my shoes back on. They felt so sticky, so uncomfortable, that I walked barefoot to my bark shelter.

Inside it was warm. The walls weren't tight enough to block the worn black sky, nor the clean smell of a clear night. I hated to think that this forest was small, but compared to the lengths it once stretched, it was. There was an end to it. There were borders. There were cigarette butts.

I tried to think which side I preferred and I couldn't remember anymore. Enough of my life had been both that I couldn't imagine one without the other.

I returned to Skye and Sandal Girl the next morning. We continued the same arrangement for the next two years. There was usually soggy hair in the drain and ants in the sink, but it was a comfortable existence. I walked across the street twice a day to play the brilliant grand pianos, and I composed a string of waltzes. All were in A-minor, except one in the key of E flat-major. I couldn't finish that one. The ending wouldn't come to me.

My next two teachers were more like Edmondson than Caroline. One of them wore a different color beret to every lesson, and the other had her nose, lip, and eyebrow pierced. Behind her thumb was a scribbled tattoo that I mistook for months as an old pen marking. It turned out to be a flower.

It was this teacher—Sara—who took one of my concertos to the school's symphony director. It was she who convinced them to perform it at the end of the year recital, with me on the piano. I wished Conner could have heard it. I had never experienced such weightlessness. The concert was recorded. Later it was played on the local classical music station. I received a call from the Steinway piano company.

"We'd like to sponsor a concert series, we were so impressed by your work," the lady said.

When I was younger I had dreamed of such a life; I had expected it.

I traveled to universities and concert halls across the country. Steinway paid for everything—hotel, food, transportation, wardrobe. In sparkling floor-length dresses I performed Chopin, Mozart, and Debussy, with my own music always saved for the illustrious finale.

All the while I inhabited some dreamworld; a world where I was so happy and fulfilled that I stopped seeing Conner's dark hair whenever I played. Two years. He was never coming back.

By day I practiced and I toured the cities. At night I sat on the stage to let the milky stars hang down over my face. The yellow streetlights didn't bother me. I thought little of the concrete hills and the dead buildings blocking the horizon.

When the contract ended I had a year's worth of performance experience, considerable savings, and a fantastic resume. But I had no idea what would come next. There was nothing ahead of me but concrete, flat and cold.

As I moved back into my parent's house, the old emptiness came again. The hazy lights fell away, as did the hushed audience voices, the lines of casual people waiting to shake my glamorous hand.

Instead there were the trees that I had forsaken. There was the moon I had barely seen through the year of smog.

Although I received commissions for a new composition every so often, it was apparent that, unless I lived with my parents indefinitely, I wouldn't be able to make my living solely as a composer. I would have to teach, or get into film music, or be hired to perform with an orchestra.

Like Hallie had done before she started teaching at our old high school, I lived at home to save up enough money for my own place. I would move to the city eventually. There would be more opportunities there.

My grandmother called. She told me that her friend had seen my last performance at the university.

"He has this great little vacation cabin," she told me, her voice pleased and uneven. "He showed me pictures. It's just darling. He thought you might want to use it if you want to get out of the city. He's in the senior living center now. He doesn't go up there anymore, his knees are so bad, so it's yours."

"Why would he give me anything? I don't even know him."

"He was so inspired by your music."

"But why would he . . ."

"Oh, that's right, that's right. I forgot to mention there's a piano inside."

I bought a sturdy, used car with my earnings. I drove it up to spend the weekend, but when I saw the great trees, the moss and wind beneath them, I decided to stay a little longer. And longer . . . and longer . . . until I forgot what reasons existed to live anywhere else.

The forest was not Conner. I had loved the trees before I knew him, and I could learn from the Earth as he had done. The forest was alive. It took deep, mourning breaths whenever I strayed from it. Conner was right about the music. It didn't come from the wind in the trees, or from the birds bellowing, as one might think; it came, instead, from all the distant, trembling rhythms; from the delicate scraping of branches between neighboring trees, or from the rolling hiss of the ferns as they danced after the full moon. Even the silence vibrated in long, powerful circles.

I saw the shadows as my own underwater world. They played against tree trunks in the late afternoon, colliding like waves, like a flickering candle. It wasn't long before I knew the trees well. I rested my head on their trunks to see how the flat spider webs made shelves between their limbs.

I walked along the paths the deer and I had worn between the waterleaf. At times I crouched behind dense salal bushes, careful to note which way the wind blew, and I watched the families of deer eat away at young plants. I saw in their brown eyes both thought and emotion. As I studied their bowed heads, a bobcat dashed into the middle of them. The deer leaped away. Before he left my sight, I saw the bobcat's yellow eyes shift toward the bush in which I was hiding. Without thinking, I nodded to him, in deep and fearful respect. Then his tall hind legs propelled him away. Leaves crunched beneath as he ran, but soon even that sound was absent. It was tenacious for a bobcat to go after a deer. I never knew if he caught one.

Months became moons, days became the heated chanting of the sun. By night I played my music for the stars. I hoped the bobcat would listen.

Hallie visited often; at least once a month. She brought me extra groceries and whatever mail I received at our parent's house.

"Look," she said, holding up a pale envelope. "You got another commission. See what you're missing out on? No one's going to remember you soon. Your glory days of performing are over, and everyone's going to forget you unless you keep up a presence . . ."

"Mom opened my mail again?"

"Well you're not there to do it. We have to see how urgent it is, if we need to bring it up to you right away." She slapped the envelope on the table and hovered behind it.

I scooped it up, read the letter, and set it back down. "Okay. Nice. I just finished writing something up last night, I'll give it to you to send."

Hallie glared at the wall. There was a brown bug crawling up it.

"I know I get on you about this every time. But I just don't think you understand how much more you could be doing. I mean, you're out here with *nothing*. There is *nothing* here. Don't you miss performing?"

"I do, I love performing. I'll go back to it someday. But right now I want to be here. I want to be here and just compose."

"In your prime years? You want to be stuck in the middle of nowhere? Hell, it's going to be winter! How are you going to handle a winter here, in the snow where no one can drive up and see you for months and months? And why . . . why would you even want—" she took a deep breath. "Okay. And let's be honest. We both know you're a better performer than composer. Follow your strengths. You didn't get that Steinway sponsorship because of your compositions—that just caught their attention. You really got it because of the way you play. You're never going to make it big just writing sheet music out here. Who will want it if you never even perform your compositions for anyone? Come back to the real world, May. Come back to us."

"I don't think you understand how the world works. And I don't mean the world where glorified paper means more than our own health, or the health of everything that sustains us. I mean this world. The real one underneath all the made-up things that have been piling up for a thousand years."

We said nothing. Hallie tore out her low bun, then braided her hair over her shoulder.

"You might as well learn a new instrument while you're

stuck out here," she said. "Want to buy my violin? It's for sale. You can already play it perfectly, anyway."

"Hallie, I practiced for weeks when no one was home. I went into your room, stole your violin, and learned a piece just so I could impress you."

She leaned against the table, both palms flat on its surface. Her make-up caked eyes dusted the floor.

"You can't sell your violin. Not unless you buy a new one," I said.

There was a knock at the door. I jumped. Hallie sat down, her mouth drawn into a low smile.

"Are Mom and Dad coming?" I asked. I drifted into the next room and opened the door.

A shapeless, blemished, wild face greeted me. His thick arms were crossed over his chest.

"Conner?" I touched my fingers to my lips. The day was cold around him. It rushed in through the open space between his body and the doorframe.

"Hallie asked me to come up here. To convince you to move back into town." His voice was no deeper than it had been before. The only change was his beard, which had grown in thick across his cheeks and chin.

"Did you find yourself?" I shifted my weight to rest my shoulder against the wall. I had already forgiven him long before. The forest had calmed all residual pain.

"I lied to you. I knew myself already. I knew who I was. But I felt that my views, my beliefs, were becoming your own before you even had a chance to discover them for yourself. I wanted you to have the opportunity I had. I wanted you to find out what was real, and you needed to be without me for that."

"Yeah right. How chivalrous of you."

"Look. It was something I needed to do. I can't even explain it, I just had to wander for a little bit. On my own, in a bath of simplicity. Everything was crumbling around me, and I kept thinking, there's this whole world out there. There's this whole other life I could be living. I needed to be a nomad, without things, without duties, without even love. Just me and the sky and the changing landscapes. Just my legs moving and building muscle, and my hair left to grow as it pleased. I wanted to see who I was in a place where I knew no one, where I was a stranger. Blank, I wanted to be blank so I could rewrite the story. I kept thinking, 'let your affairs be as one or two, not a hundred or a thousand'."

"Who said that, again?"

"Thoreau," he said. "But I didn't . . . it turns out I already knew who I was. My life was already simple. There's very little in this world that's real anymore, and once you break the spell, it's obvious. Painfully obvious what sustains us, what fulfills us. There was this hollowness to everything I saw, like it wasn't as colorful as it could be. And I realized it was because you weren't there. And, May, that took me too long to realize. I'm sorry. I can't say it enough."

I said nothing.

Conner spoke. "I wrote song for you," he said.

"A piece, you mean. Unless it has lyrics."

Conner shook his head until his hair swung across his forehead. We were silent. Silence was always easy, between us. He stepped inside.

"This is nice."

"Everyone is always telling me to leave here," I said softly. "They've been telling me since the day I got here that I need to come back. They don't like me being up here alone."

"If they're so worried about you being alone, why don't they offer to stay here with you?"

"I guess they're all too afraid. They want TV and paved roads and shopping malls. They don't care about wild streams, or birdsongs. They don't care about music."

Conner touched my cheek, his eyes closer to mine than they had ever been.

And he sat down at the piano to play his piece. It was as though I was listening to myself from afar, a ghost in a pale dream. The tempo was slow and bitter, but the notes themselves sang of life. It was, without a doubt, a nocturne.

As the music drifted out the window's glass, and melted over the wooden floors of the house, I realized that the oak tree outside the house could hear him play.

So could the cedars, and the bobcat, too, lounging beneath their dancing shadows. So could the cattails down by the stream, and the family of robins who lived in the maple branch.

All that lived in the forest heard him play and absorbed the movement of his music into their being. And they would carry that with them, into their wind-blown seed, or their tiny blue egg, which would again grow, and again hear the echoes of that very nocturne. With Conner next to me, with the cold wind still rushing in from the open door—I realized that as long as the forest stood, we would live forever.

# About the Author

Francesca G. Varela was raised in Oregon's Willamette Valley. Her dream of becoming an author began in third grade, and her writing career had an early start; she had a poem published in the 2002 edition of *The Anthology of Poetry by Young Americans*. Her debut novel, *Call of the Sun Child,* won the Bronze Medal in the 2014 Moonbeam Children's Book Awards for Best First Book and also was named a Finalist in the 2015 Next Generation Indie Book Awards in the Young Adult category. She recently graduated from the University of Oregon with degrees in Environmental Studies and Creative Writing. When not writing, she spends her time practicing piano and violin, figure skating, walking her dog, Ginger, and exploring Oregon's wild places.

# HOMEBOUND PUBLICATIONS

*Ensuring that the mainstream isn't the only stream.*

At Homebound Publications, we publish books written by independent voices for independent minds. Our books focus on a return to simplicity and balance, connection to the earth and each other, and the search for meaning and authenticity. Founded in 2011, Homebound Publications is one of the rising independent publishers in the country. Collectively through our imprints, we publish between fifteen to twenty offerings each year. Our authors have received dozens of awards, including: Foreword Review Book of the Year, Nautilus Book Award, Benjamin Franklin Book Awards, and Saltire Literary Awards. Highly-respected among bookstores, readers and authors alike, Homebound Publications has a proven devotion to quality, originality and integrity.

We are a small press with big ideas. As an independent publisher we strive to ensure that the mainstream is not the only stream. It is our intention at Homebound Publications to preserve contemplative storytelling. We publish full-length introspective works of creative non-fiction as well as essay collections, travel writing, poetry, and novels. In all our titles, our intention is to introduce new perspectives that will directly aid humankind in the trials we face at present as a global village.

WWW.HOMEBOUNDPUBLICATIONS.COM

CPSIA information can be obtained
at www.ICGtesting.com
Printed in the USA
LVHW04s1134260718
584949LV00001B/93/P